WAY TO GO, TEDDY

Weekly Reader Children's Book Club presents

WAY TO GO, TEDDY

•

by Donald Honig

WEEKLY READER
CHILDREN'S BOOK CLUB
This is a registered trademark

Franklin Watts, Inc. · New York · 1973

Library of Congress Cataloging in Publication Data

Honig, Donald.
    Way to go, Teddy.

    SUMMARY: Entering professional baseball against
his father's will, Ted seems unable to maintain an honest relationship with his father as his batting average
first soars and then continually drops.
    [1. Baseball—Stories. 2. Fathers and sons—
Fiction] I. Title.
PZ7.H748Way   [Fic]   72-8494
ISBN 0-531-02604-3

Design by Diana Hrisinko

Weekly Reader Children's Book Club Edition

For
MILDRED ELSON HONIG

WAY TO GO, TEDDY

· 1 ·

THERE WAS SNOW ON THE PITCHER'S MOUND, SNOW IN THE batter's box, snow on the infield, and snow on the outfield. The sky was a dead gray and the wind was sharp and icy. The wooden grandstands behind the dugouts were empty and the trees beyond the grandstands had long streaks of snow balanced along their skinned-off branches.

Every so often during the winter we hiked down the road to the high school and walked on the baseball diamond. Once we got there, it somehow didn't matter that it was covered with snow. Just walking on the field made us feel close to baseball, to summer. Just walking on the field could bring back the games of last summer, the sweet smell of the grass, the sound of a well-hit baseball, the shouts of the infielders yelling encouragement to the pitcher. It was as if the magic never left the place where baseball was played and all you had to do to be part of it again was to walk on the field, and never mind the snow.

We walked from home plate, across the infield and into the outfield, our boots crunching the hard-packed snow. We were both wearing parkas with the hoods up and when you turned a certain way you could hear the wind whistling around your ears inside the hood.

"Well," Bill said, "I guess you won't be playing here next year."

"I hope not," I said.

"They're going to miss you. My father said you're the best ballplayer this town's turned out in twenty years."

"Your father said that?" I was pleased to hear that, because Bill's father had played minor league ball for a few years after the war, and when it came to baseball knew what he was talking about. But at the same time, I couldn't help feeling a little bit sad.

"I wish my father would say that," I said.

"Your father thinks you're a good ballplayer," Bill said.

We were walking around the outfield, our hands in our pockets, our hooded heads bent, little puffs of vapor coming from our mouths every time we breathed.

"Oh, sure," I said. "He doesn't mind coming out to watch me play—now and then on Sunday."

"In pro ball you play every day," Bill said, like he was describing a dream.

"Mostly night games too," I said.

"And people paying money to watch you."

"And us getting *paid* to play."

Bill shook his head. "I wish somebody'd offer me a contract," he said. "There'd be no problem. My father would be out of his head with excitement. . . ."

We walked back across the infield and sat on the ice-cold wooden bench in the dugout, tapping our feet up and down to keep them warm. The field looked like a cold white desert; it was hard to believe that all the snow could ever melt, warm sunshine would come again, and the grass would grow when spring came and turn the field green.

"What's your father got against you playing pro ball anyway?" Bill asked.

"He wants me to go on to college. He says I can play ball there."

"And after you get out?"

"Become a lawyer, like him."

Bill didn't say anything. I knew what he was thinking —what a terrible predicament this was for me. He knew what I wanted to do, and he knew, too, that because I was only seventeen I couldn't sign the contract without my father's permission.

"He doesn't want you to play ball at all?" he asked after we'd sat quietly for a little while blowing puffs of steam onto the cold air.

"Not professionally," I said.

"I don't figure it," he said shaking his head. "There are guys who'd give anything for the chance. Doesn't he know that? Doesn't he know that if you make it big you'll make more money than any lawyer?"

"That's not the way he figures. He said there are thousands of guys who go into baseball for every one who makes it big."

"But you can hit, Teddy. I mean, you can *really* hit."

Well, that was true, I suppose. But all I had hit against so far was sandlot and high school pitching, where you seldom see anything more than a decent fast ball. I believed I was a pretty good hitter, but you can never tell until you face professional pitching, swinging against guys who not only threw the big fast ball but had the curve to go with it as well as good pitching sense to back them up.

I wanted my chance to see how good I was at what I loved to do, and what other people thought I did pretty well. It seemed to me that it was only fair. I was even willing to make a deal with my father: If I did poorly after two years I would quit pro ball and go to college. He didn't buy the idea. He said that once a fellow's education has been interrupted he seldom goes back. He said that going into pro ball was too big a gamble, and not worth the risk.

The day my high school class graduated the scout came around wanting to sign me. I'd had the feeling all summer and fall that it was going to happen. You know when they're watching you. I think I could pick out a scout from a thousand people at a ball game.

I'd seen this fellow come to games three Sundays in a row during July. In a small town like ours, tucked away into the mountains up there in New England, you take note of strangers—especially after the local papers have been running your name all over the sports pages and saying what a great prospect you are. You just *know* that sooner or later a big league scout is going to turn up. It's almost like the law of gravity or something.

When he showed up on that third Sunday in a row he sat down in the wooden bleachers and never took his eyes off me. I was so keyed up I felt as if I was going to step right into the big leagues the next morning. You get those crazy feelings, just because there's somebody in town who's got a *connection* with a big league team.

I'd been praying all week for sun, the same as farmers in the Southwest pray for rain when there's been a drought. And you never saw such sunshine as that day; it was being just poured out of the sky like a yellow waterfall. I said to Bill, "Keep your eye on that guy. I think he's a scout."

Sure enough, after I'd hit a long line drive to right center the scout didn't watch the ball or the right fielder like everybody else, but kept his eyes on me to see how fast I could dig around the bases. That's what Bill told me later: Never took his eyes off me.

After the game he came around and introduced himself. His name was Jack Wilburt and he worked this part of New England for the club. He asked me when I was graduating high school, what my plans for the future were, and so on. Scouts are not allowed to talk real business with you until you or your class has graduated from high school, so the conversation was strictly limited. But I knew what he was thinking and he knew what I was thinking.

That night was when the trouble started. It should have been the happiest day of my life, but at the same time I should have anticipated my father's reaction. Every so often I had mentioned the hope of playing pro ball after high school, and each time I did he sort of looked at me funny, the same way he did when I put too much salt on my food.

When I came home (actually I charged through the front door like I was scoring the winning run in the last of the ninth) and told Mom and Dad about the scout, my father gave me that look, shook his head, and said, "I'm proud of you, Ted, but you're going to college."

My mother said, "Let's see what happens."

My kid brother Eddie said, "A big league scout!"

Because it was a touchy subject, nothing much was said about it for a long time. But it was always right there under the surface. When my father started talking about colleges and a career in law, I really had to strain to pretend interest. He saw I wasn't paying serious attention and I knew it annoyed him. He wasn't one to fool around when it came to talking about the future. He said that a person had only so much time to make a success for himself and that if the time were wasted the person would have nothing but a lifetime of regret. He was probably right, though I never really discussed it with him; I didn't like to think in big chunks of time the way he did.

The day after I graduated high school Jack Wilburt came to the house. My father told him I'd already been accepted by the state university and that was that. But I said I wanted to sign the contract. Jack Wilburt didn't want to get into the middle of a family argument, so he said he'd call back in a week for a final answer. He had the contract right in his pocket, too, which was a real killer.

"So he's coming back tomorrow, huh?" Bill said.

We were still sitting in the dugout, our feet still tapping up and down on the snow-packed wooden floor.

"Yeah," I said. "He's driving over from Manchester. That's where he lives."

"And he's going to have the contract with him?"

"Sure."

"And your father's not going to sign it?"

I shrugged. I didn't know. I sat there looking out at the field, the old ball field, all covered over with snow. All I knew was that if I wasn't able to have my chance at pro ball, then that field and all fields, might just as well stay covered with snow forever.

· 2 ·

IT WAS MY MOTHER WHO SAID TO ME, "YOU HAVE TO TRY TO understand your father."

Well, I tried. I spent one whole afternoon in my room thinking about my father. First I pretended I was his age, figuring that would help. But it didn't. No matter how old I made myself, he still somehow came out older when I started to think. Then I tried making him my age, but that didn't work either. I tried thinking that he wasn't my father, that he was just some man I knew who had peculiar ideas, and tried to look at the world the way he did. He came out pretty strict in that line of thought, so I dropped it.

I tried to see him from every angle, inside out, upside down, hoping to learn what made him think and act the way he did, searching out every possible reason. Look, I told myself, your father's no dummy. He's a bright guy and he loves you and wants the best for you. He's not just a stubborn and thick-headed man who wants to have his own way. He always said that an important decision made without plenty of thought was a fool's choice. I liked that, and told him so. I told him, too, that I had given pro baseball plenty of thought and had my good reasons for wanting to play. But not even that made him like the idea.

Now, look, I told myself, be honest. Give the man a break. So I went over all that I knew about him. (It's a thing of shock sometimes when you realize how little thought you've given to your own parents, especially to them being people and not just your parents.) I knew he'd come from a very poor family, had worked his way through school, started his own law practice in a tiny office, and now had the biggest practice in town. He was very proud of his achievements and wanted my brother and me to follow in his footsteps.

Well, that's his life story, leaving out a few details here and there. I loved him and was proud of him, but I didn't want to be a lawyer—at least not yet.

So you can't say that I didn't try to understand my father, just as my mother had asked me to. I tried, and I think I *did* understand him a little. In fact, I think I understood him a lot. It was just that we didn't agree, that's all.

There was tension when I walked into the house. I unlaced my wet boots and left them on the straw mat in the hall. I found my father sitting in the living room reading the paper. But after a minute or so I got the feeling he wasn't reading the paper, but rather holding it and looking at it. I could feel him thinking—and guess what about?

My mother came in and smiled and said dinner would be ready in a half hour. Her smile was brave. She had sort of a pained look. She was somewhere in the middle as far as the big question was concerned. For my mother it would have been perfect if I could have played baseball in the afternoon and gone to college at night.

I sat across from my father, watching him look at the newspaper. After about ten minutes he still hadn't turned the page (and he was a fast reader). Then he put the paper down in his lap, raised his hand to his face, and lifted off his glasses.

"I was looking for you this afternoon," he said.

Since I wasn't starting college until the fall (I'd stalled around long enough to miss the winter enrollments, hoping for that baseball contract), my father wanted me to put in as much time around the office as I could, to sort of get the feel of what it was like to be a lawyer. But I'd been keeping away; not that I minded hanging around the office, but just so that he didn't think I was making a commitment, if you know what I mean.

"I was up to the ball field," I said.

"In the dead of winter?"

"I like to go there."

"Trying to relive your days of glory, eh?" he asked with a little smile.

Maybe to somebody else, a ball fan, for instance, I could have explained what I felt on a baseball diamond, even in the dead of winter. It wasn't to relive any glory, but to keep in touch—that's the best way I can explain it. You go out there and it sort of refreshes you and feeds the desire. That thing someplace inside you that makes you want to play baseball, needs to know that you're walking on a ball field again.

My kid brother walked in then. Eddie was fourteen. He loved to play ball too, but he had absolutely no talent. I don't think he was able to hit a pitched ball until he was nine years old, and when he did he got so excited that he ran the bases the wrong way. So he was no threat to the family happiness.

Eddie had a big grin on his face when he saw me. He was as excited about the scout coming tomorrow as I was. But when he saw my father sitting there the smile went away and his face became as neutral as a stone.

"Hi," he said.

"Hello, Ed," my father said.

I gave him a wink, which meant get lost. And he did. It's great when brothers can communicate without saying anything. I think that sort of thing develops between brothers when they find the old man tough to talk to.

When my father and I were alone again he got up, his hands patting the sides of his tweed jacket. That meant he was looking for his pipe and tobacco. As he poked around the room and found them, then proceeded to load his pipe and light it, I knew the time had come for the showdown. He seemed to need the pipe in his hand when he got down to serious talk. (He once said to me that if he could smoke in a courtroom he'd never lose a case.)

"Come into my study, Ted," he said.

I followed him into the study and he closed the door. The room was all wood and leather and carpeting and books. Nobody was allowed in there except for special events. I knew that was what this was going to be.

He sat down on the edge of the desk, puffing his pipe and staring at me. I stared back, figuring I had better show him I wasn't afraid, that I was sure of my own mind. You don't gain anything by not looking right square back at people you're having a serious talk with.

He was a good guy, really. But I always thought of Bill once saying, "Hey, why does your old man always wear a tie and jacket in the house?" What could I say? That's the way my father was. I guess it was because he was a lawyer and knew that people liked their lawyers to be neat and serious. Nobody would want a lawyer who walked around the house in his underwear and made bad jokes. My father was a handsome man, tall, smooth-haired, and built rangy like a good-fielding shortstop (though he never played ball, was never athletic in any way, except for bowling, if that counts).

"Ted," he said, "if a stranger came into the house and tried to break up the family, you'd be pretty upset, wouldn't you?"

"Sure," I said.

"Well, this is what's happened."

"You mean Mr. Wilburt, the scout?" I asked.

"No I don't mean him at all. I'm talking about something else. I'm talking about baseball."

"Baseball?"

"It's come into this house and upset and divided this family."

"But it's not a stranger," I said. "I've been playing ball since I was a kid."

"Yes, and you're no longer a kid. You're on the verge of becoming an adult. Wanting to play professional baseball is like an attempt to prolong your childhood. Don't you see?"

"No, I don't. Professional baseball is played by grown men."

"Yes, but only on the highest levels. And those levels are reached by the merest handful—you yourself have said that. My point is, that by the time you've found out that you're not going to be one of the handful, you could have damaged your future to a serious extent."

"But nobody knows unless he tries," I said.

"Isn't it better to go into law, where you *know* you're going to be one of the best?"

"How can I know that?"

"Because you'll get a good education, then come to work for me. In due time you'll take over the practice, and you'll be the best in this town. And who knows—law has been the springboard into greater things for many men."

I knew what he meant. A lot of presidents and governors and senators had been lawyers. And even if I didn't go that far, then he'd see to it that I was the best lawyer in town. The best, nothing but the best. That's what he believed in. He seemed to have this terrific fear of failing, of not being the best. That's probably why he never went in for athletics himself, not even on the sandlot level. Why failing and not being the best seemed to him to be the same thing was something I couldn't understand.

For a minute—less, a split second—I was going to tell him all right, call Mr. Wilburt and tell him not to come, I won't sign, I won't play ball. Because I hated what was happening between my father and me. We'd always been good friends, but baseball had gotten in the way and lately there was always that tension.

But I caught myself right up, feeling scared for what I'd *almost* said.

"Why can't I have my chance?"

"Because I think it's a mistake," he said. "Finish college first."

"I'll be too old then."

"Too old?" He smiled.

"I might not want to play then."

"So?"

"Then I might be sorry for the rest of my life."

"You could be sorry if you do play."

"At least it'll be my own fault," I said.

"I'm not signing that contract for you," he said. He

got off of the desk now and sat down in his leather swivel chair behind it and stared at me, like a judge.

I couldn't believe it. I really couldn't.

"It's not fair," I muttered. "Everybody says I can make it. It's not fair."

"But it's right."

"You don't know."

"I'm not happy about this, Ted, believe me."

"When I was five years old you bought me a ball and glove."

"Every father does that. What did you expect, a briefcase?"

"Maybe you should have bought me that, if you were going to plan my whole life for me without giving me a chance to say anything about it."

Now he got quiet. I guess he didn't like the sound of that. He gazed down at the glass-topped desk for a while, puffing on his pipe. Then he looked up at me.

"It's my responsibility as your father to guide you," he said.

"For how long?" I asked.

"For as long as I'm legally able to."

"But what happens to my talent?" I asked. I was getting scared.

"Your talent?"

"Yes," I said. "It's a real talent, just like anything else —like painting or acting or . . . or . . . even being a lawyer. Hitting a baseball, and running, and throwing

. . . those are talents too. What am I supposed to do with them?"

"Can't you play ball in college?"

"It's not the same. It wouldn't be good."

"But why?"

Then I said something that sounded like bragging, but which I guess I really meant.

"Because the competition isn't sharp enough. I'm too *good* to play that brand of ball."

He frowned at me, sitting back in the chair, holding the pipe in his mouth with his hand. I swear he stared at me for five minutes; it seemed like that long anyhow.

"You think you're that good?" he asked, not as if he doubted me but like he was interested, curious.

"I think so," I said, staring right back at him.

"You seem to have a lot of confidence in yourself."

"I can't help it, it's the way I feel."

"Don't apologize for it," he said. "You've got to feel confidence in yourself. Without it, you're nothing. Because if you go out to play ball you're not going to be the best unless you believe you can be. And that's what you're going to have to be—the best. Nothing less will do. There's no substitute for it. No substitute whatsoever."

"You mean I can sign the contract?" I asked.

Very seriously, he nodded his head.

"We'll see if you're as good as you think you are," he said.

I wished he would have smiled when he said it.

· 3 ·

On my fifth day in spring training camp i got picked up by the police, and that was really something, because it's true what you hear about cops in little southern towns—they can be pretty tough. I thought for sure my career was over, right then and there, even before it started.

My father drove me to Boston, from where I caught a plane to Florida. All the way to Boston he kept telling me to work hard, never let up for a minute, don't let anybody else do better, and things like that. I shook hands goodbye at the airport in five degrees of bone-rattling freezing weather, and a few hours later stepped out into a sultry ninety degrees of Florida sunshine—wearing an overcoat and two sweaters.

I don't think I was ever more depressed than I was on the first day of spring training. Suddenly I had a look at the competition—and in spring training that's what everybody is. You don't have teammates until after the cutdown. Until that time everybody is competing for a place on the squad.

The team I was signed for carried only seventeen or

eighteen players during the regular season. They carry that few in the low minors in order to give everybody a chance to play. There's no point in having a minor leaguer sitting on the bench, when the whole purpose of the minors is to see what a guy can do.

I was in a training camp in central Florida with the squads of two other teams—a grand total of about a hundred players. That meant more than thirty guys trying out for each team. It wasn't the quantity of the competition that bothered me, it was the quality. I tell you, the minute I walked out onto the field and had a look at the other players, I got depressed. It wasn't that they were doing anything more than lobbing balls back and forth and just loosening up; it was the way they *looked,* the way they handled themselves. It was altogether different from the first day of tryouts for the high school team, where just by looking you can tell that most of the guys aren't very good ballplayers. There's a certain way a man *stands* and *moves* on a ballfield that can tell you an awful lot about his ability.

Everybody on the field under that hot sun had been a star in his hometown. Each guy had been all-state or all-city or all-something, and had the confidence of having been the best. You could tell just by watching them throw a ball back and forth. And you didn't see any low throws getting away. On the sandlots you always see a guy chasing a ball he couldn't handle; here, they were scooping them up, back-handing them out of the dirt, just as easy as pie.

Well, I figured, I was all-state too. I'd been a star in high school, and I'd hit that crumby pitching for .500. So I punched the pocket of my glove and said to myself, Hell, let *them* worry about *me*.

Spring training is real hard work, and I took it seriously, which I guess is why I got arrested. But I'm coming to that. They really work you. And under that hot sun. All of a sudden I could feel the long, lazy winter in my bones, trying to soak itself out. Those first few days all we did was calisthenics, running, and a little light throwing. They had calisthenics you never dreamed about. There was one that everybody hated, called the rocker. You lie down on your belly and fold your hands behind you and rock back and forth. If the coaches don't like the way you're doing it one of them comes over and takes you by the ankles and shakes you back and forth like a seesaw.

But more than anything else, we ran. The first thing you learn is always to run on a baseball field. That's what our manager, Ken Pulski, told us the first day of camp. He was a big guy, built like a tank, and though he looked tough he was really a very gentle man. He never raised his voice, but he had small shrewd eyes that didn't miss a trick. He'd played ball in the high minors, never making it to the bigs. He was about forty years old.

"Boys," he told us that first day, "once you suit up and step out onto a ballfield, you've got to hustle. There's no other way. If you don't hustle, the upshot will be that people will think you're lazy. And the upshot of that will be a mark against you."

That seemed to be his favorite word, "upshot." After two days the guys started calling him—not to his face, of course—"Mr. Upshot."

We lived in a long, low, barracks-type building right near the three diamonds where we worked out every day. The nearby town, Opeko, was all of two blocks long and there wasn't much doing there. The town didn't even have a movie. After dinner we walked in for a soda, stood around on the corner for a while waiting for a car to go by, then headed back home. There was a rec hall next to the barracks and it had a Coke machine and a juke box and that was where most of the guys hung out at night. Night-life was pretty slow going in Opeko. As one of the guys said, we were "spared from temptation."

After five days of hard workouts I wasn't satisfied with the shape I was in. They were going to start inter-squad games in another day or so, which meant I'd be looking at some good pitching, and here I was, still tight through the shoulders and legs.

I mentioned this to one of the guys. His name was Mike Delaney, a pitcher, from a little town in Ohio. He had the bunk next to mine in the barracks and we'd become friends on the first day. I liked him right off because he had a real friendly manner, was quick to laugh and joke, and always had a lookout for mischief in his eye.

"There's a way to beat this system, Teddy boy," he said to me one night. It was after dinner and we were lying on our cots.

"What system?" I asked.

"Look at it this way," he said, getting up on one elbow and looking at me. He had red hair, which he wore kind of long, and a few freckles on his nose, which seemed to light up when he smiled. "It's all a matter of time, right? There's time to get into shape, time to play ball, time to show what you can do. Now, if most of the guys are of equal ability, and everybody gets the same chance to play, how do they decide who to keep and who to cut?"

"By performance," I said. "If I hit, they've got to keep me."

"But suppose you're a good hitter and by some freak of things you don't hit?"

"Why shouldn't I hit?" I asked.

"Because you might be slow rounding into shape. Time is the big thing," he said poking the air with his finger. "We all have the same amount of time out on the field, right?"

"Right."

"So it's all equal. Right?"

"Right," I said.

"Wrong," he said all of a sudden.

"What the devil are you talking about?"

Now he got up and sat on the edge of his cot and bent

close and started talking in a low voice, not that there was anybody within earshot. Most of the guys were either outside or in the rec hall.

"You know what my father said to me when I left home?" he said. "He told me that if I got into shape I'd make it. Getting into the best possible physical shape is everything, especially when you have only a few weeks to show what you can do."

"So what are you worried about? I've noticed you're doing all right."

He was, too. He was the only pitcher who'd gone four laps around the field so far. In spring training they run the pitchers right into the ground, because a pitcher's legs are as important as his arm. If his legs aren't good, then it doesn't matter if he's got an arm like a cannon— he's going to get tired and lose his efficiency.

"I'm running better than any pitcher in camp," he said. "When the games start I'm going to be in the best shape of any pitcher here. That's like having a head start."

"That's right," I said.

"You know why you're still stiff?"

"Why?"

"Because you think everything is equal."

"There you go again," I said. "I don't know what you're talking about."

He laughed. Then he grew serious again.

"I've been stealing time," he said.

"You're still not making sense. How do you steal time?"

"You want to do it?"

I nodded.

"Our secret?" he asked.

I raised my right hand, like I was taking an oath.

"I'll show you tonight," he said.

Then he lay down on his cot again, looking at me with a big foolish grin on his face.

Curfew was eleven o'clock, and soon after that there was a bedcheck. The bedcheck was made by one of the coaches, who came walking through the barracks smoking a cigar, looking at every cot. He never spoke to anybody and nobody ever spoke to him, and there was just this silent thing every night—this guy with the cigar walking through and looking at everybody.

Soon after the bedcheck the lights went out and the whole camp settled in for a night's sleep. Everybody, that is, except Mike Delaney. What he was doing each night was getting out of bed, getting dressed, and slipping out of the barracks. Then he headed for town and began running. That's exactly what he did: he started running, in and out of the back streets of Opeko, along the main highway, sometimes in and out of the orange groves that bordered the highway. He would run for about an hour, then slip back into the barracks and go to sleep. This was how he was "stealing time"—by doing this extra running.

"Why don't you run on the diamonds?" I asked.

"Too close to home," he said. "You never know when Upshot or some of the others might be walking around."

"They might admire your enthusiasm."

"They don't admire *anything* you do after curfew, kiddo," he said. "And besides, I don't want any of the guys to know what I'm doing either. Why give away the secrets of your success?"

So that night we waited until bedcheck was over and the guys had quieted down and gone to sleep. Then we got out of bed, got dressed, and slipped out of the barracks.

It wasn't until we were outside in the soft Florida night that I realized what a dumb thing we were doing. The team was very serious about discipline; one of the first things they stressed to us when camp started was to observe the curfew, and they would be very unhappy with anybody who broke it. But Mike had been doing it every night and not been caught, so I figured we could get away with it.

It was a funny feeling, being out when you weren't supposed to be. Even though it was for a good cause, I still had this curious, *guilty* feeling, like we were thieves or something (though I guess thieves don't feel that way).

If the town was quiet at the height of the evening, you can imagine what it was like after midnight. The stores were closed, the streets were more than empty— they looked deserted, as if nobody was ever coming back.

Walking away from the direction of the camp, we

crossed the main drag of Opeko and entered a side street. There was a full moon and in its light we could see the tropical trees lining the sidewalk and behind them rows of unattached, bungalow-type houses. There wasn't a light on in any of the houses. Even though I come from a small town myself, I still wasn't sure of the answer to this question: Is a town quiet at night because everybody goes to bed early, or does everybody go to bed early because the town is quiet?

Once we were in the side street we began jogging. We ran in the middle of the street, since there was no traffic. Mike looked at me with that silly grin of his, like a kid sharing his mischief.

"Stretch those legs, boy," he said. "You're in spring training. Limber up. Got to make the team."

"Shut up," I said. "You're not supposed to talk when you run. It takes the wind out of you."

So we jogged along, our sneakers slapping softly on the black-topped road. It felt good. Running under the hot sun can really take the juice out of you, but jogging along in the cool night air it felt just fine. Once or twice Mike let out the throttle and for a few hundred feet or so we sprinted. He thought he was fast, and he was; but I was faster. I never really opened up all the way, but each time I left him behind.

We cut in and out of the back streets, sailing along under the star-filled Florida sky, past the sleeping bungalows and palm trees, stretching those winter-locked muscles.

I was thinking what a great idea this was, when all of a sudden a light picked us up in the middle of the street. Without breaking stride, we turned around and saw a car coming. And it wasn't just headlights on us; there was a blazing spotlight off the roof of the car.

"That's the cops!" Mike yelled.

· 4 ·

You do dumb things when you're scared; or maybe you're scared because you're doing a dumb thing. Whatever it was, we took off like a couple of shots out of a cannon, trying to outrun a police car. Mike Delaney found speed in his feet he didn't know he had; in fact, there was a moment when he even passed me, and I was going full blast.

We were so scared that we stayed right in the middle of the street. If we'd had any sense, we would have cut away from the street and run through some back yards and try to lose them that way. Though if we'd had any *real* sense, we wouldn't have been out there in the first place.

The next thing we knew the lights were all over us and the car had pulled up alongside and a rough voice with a southern drawl was saying,

"Right there, boys."

We stopped. So did the car. The door opened and the driver got out, leaving the motor running and the lights blazing on down the road. A second man got out on the other side and walked around through the lights. This one, the second one, was wearing a badge that had "Sheriff" printed on it. Both men were wearing open-throated tan shirts and khaki slacks. Each one was tall, and lean as a fungo bat. Each one had his hands on his hips, and under each right hand was a pistol in a holster. The sheriff was wearing a white cowboy hat with the brim curled up front and back. The other man, the deputy, was hatless.

"Get against the car," the deputy said. He sounded weary, like he'd just woken up.

We leaned against the car with our hands and they searched us. Then they told us to get in.

"We didn't do anything," Mike said.

"Then why're you running in the middle of the night?" the deputy asked.

The sheriff wasn't saying much. He was just standing by with his hands on his hips, the right one just over the handle of the pistol, and chewing on something and staring at us with pinched little eyes that had lots of wrinkles in the corners.

"We were just working out," I said.

The deputy sighed, as if he'd heard the greatest lie ever. The sheriff snapped his fingers twice, like a dog trainer.

"Get in the car," the deputy said to us.

I was going to say something, ask them what it was all about. But I could see from the looks on their faces that they weren't having any more conversation. We got into the car.

They drove us to the police station. It was in a low, brick building about a quarter of a mile from the town's business district. The building served as the sheriff's office as well as the jail. When we walked in I could see behind the office a corridor with cells on either side. That's when I really started to get scared. I wondered if you were allowed to play ball if you had a criminal record. I was so scared I nearly asked if I could call my father, before I realized he was the *last* person I wanted to know about this. And the next to last person was Upshot.

We were told to sit down on a beat-up old wooden bench that stood against the wall. Then the sheriff dragged a chair across the floor and placed it in front of us, put one foot up on the seat and leaned forward with his arm across his thigh and stared at us with those little eyes with the wrinkled corners, the curled-brim hat pushed back on his thin, silvery hair.

"Now, what were you fellows doing out there?" he asked.

"Working out," Mike said.

"We're with the ballclub," I said.

"That so?" the sheriff said. "Since when does the team work its players in the middle of the street after midnight?" He didn't wait for an answer, but looked over his shoulder at the deputy and said, "Curtis, were there any calls about break-ins tonight?"

"No," the deputy said. "Just that call about these two acting peculiar."

"Break-ins?" I asked. "Say, is that what you think?"

"Look," Mike said, "you can check easy enough. Just call Mr. Pulski—he's our manager."

"Hey, don't do that," I said, not to the sheriff but to Mike. "We're not supposed to be out, remember? We could get into trouble."

"We *are* in trouble," Mike said.

"I mean *real* trouble—with the team."

I'd been looking at Mike. All of a sudden I felt a hand take my chin and turn my head until I was looking at the sheriff.

"You *got* real trouble, sonny," he said, letting go of my chin. The look in his eye was definitely unfriendly.

"We weren't doing anything but running," Mike said.

"We don't like strangers running in our streets in the middle of the night, sonny. It tends to wake up our dogs. Right, Curtis?" the sheriff asked without looking around.

"Right, Sheriff!" the deputy yelled.

"But we didn't break any law," I said. "We were just trying to get in some extra work. Honest. That's all."

Now the deputy said, "We could check with the ball-club, Sheriff."

"Being ballplayers don't necessarily make them honest," the sheriff said.

But I think he was beginning to believe our story, because he said then he wasn't going to arrest us or charge us with anything, but would keep us there until morning, to wait and see if any burglary reports came in. If none did, then he'd let us go.

"But we've got to be back by seven o'clock," Mike said.

"Don't sweat it, sonny," the sheriff said.

So we sat there. We just sat on that bench all night, hour after hour, while the sheriff dozed in a chair and the deputy sat with his feet up on the desk reading a magazine.

It occurred to me that if by some chance there was a break-in somewhere in Opeko tonight we'd be in real trouble. The phone did ring once and I thought I'd hit the ceiling, but it was only the deputy's wife calling to tell him to stop at the bakery on his way home in the morning.

Whenever the deputy turned a page of the magazine he'd look over at us and say, "Comfortable?"

One of us would answer, "No."

And he'd go right on reading.

The night seemed to last forever, endless and boring and filled with tension. I couldn't help thinking of all the things that could happen to us, from going to jail to being banned from baseball. And even if we were let off at sunup, we'd be playing ball tomorrow on exactly no hours sleep.

Somewhere around five-thirty the sheriff woke up.

"Any calls?" he asked the deputy.

"Nothing," the deputy said.

The sheriff looked at us.

"Lucky boys," he said.

● 33 ●

At six o'clock they made coffee and gave us each a cup. Then, at about six-thirty, the sheriff told us to take off.

"Stay outa trouble now, y'hear?" he said.

When we got outside into the morning sunshine we had no choice but to trot back to the barracks, even though we were dead tired.

"Little extra workout," Mike said.

"Shut up," I said.

When we got back to the barracks we slipped in through a side door. I looked enviously at all the guys, so peacefully asleep, so rested.

We undressed and got into our cots. Not until my head touched the pillow did I realize how really tired I was. I closed my eyes and fell right to sleep. I could have slept for twelve hours, but all I got was about five minutes, because that's when Adam came in, yelling. We called him Adam because he came in every morning yelling, "Up and at 'em, up and at 'em!"

I sat up slowly. My head felt as if it were under water, while my eyes felt like they were on fire. I looked across at Mike. He was up on one elbow, grinning at me.

"Good morning, sonny," he said. "Sleep well?"

· 5 ·

THEY MADE A MOVIE ONCE ABOUT THE D-DAY INVASION and called it "The Longest Day." But they were wrong; the day after we had been picked up was the longest day.

I suited up and went in for breakfast, then went out onto the field with the other guys. I felt like a zombie. I was so sleepy I couldn't hear—that's the truth. Words and noises sounded like they were coming from miles away.

I fumbled through a game of pepper, did some running, some shagging, and felt like I was going to collapse any moment. Then came the big news: there was going to be a game that afternoon, the first of the training season. All of the guys were excited; it was what everybody had been waiting for—a chance to show what they could do in real competition.

Mike sat down next to me during lunch. His eyes looked like they had been bathed in tomato juice.

"Pray for rain," he said.

Well, it didn't rain, and we played the game. As luck would have it, they batted me fourth on my squad, right smack in the clean-up spot, where I was expected to be the big hitter.

The first time I stepped into the batter's box, the bat felt like a telephone pole in my hand. Some guys can look good striking out. I didn't even achieve that much. My timing was way off and I swung with all the style and crispness of a revolving door. The sad thing was, the pitcher didn't have a thing—he was throwing meatballs and everybody else was hitting screamers all over the place.

In the field I prayed nobody would hit anything my way. I felt as if I was standing up to my hips in water, and I moved the same way. Luck was with me here, though. I had only one chance and it was an easy one, a popup into short center, which I handled okay.

Next time at bat I looked even worse. This time the bat felt like a tree. I couldn't even wait out a walk, since they were playing no walks, wanting to give everybody a chance to hit. But they were playing strikeouts, and I chalked up another one.

I was sitting in the dugout when I felt a friendly pat on the back.

"You'll do better tomorrow, sonny," Mike said.

"You pitching?" I asked.

"I asked to be scrubbed," he said. "Told them I had an upset stomach."

"Why you miserable scheming—"

He laughed.

The only break I got all day was when they changed squads in the middle of the game, to give more guys a chance to get in. As I was leaving the field and heading for the shower, walking with my head down, I heard a stern voice say a single word:

"Run." It was Pulski, the skipper. I looked at him and then forced myself into a trot to the showers. Instead of refreshing me, the shower was like a lullaby and I swear I fell asleep twice under the water.

That night, after dinner, I was worried. I was sitting up in the empty grandstands looking down at the field. And I had the miserable feeling that, after today's performance, this was where I belonged—sitting up there. A hitter was supposed to hit, no matter what. So what if I missed a night's sleep? That shouldn't have had anything to do with it. A real hitter can pound that ball even if he's unconscious, so they say.

I knew you didn't get many chances here, and that sometimes first impressions stuck. I was marked down now as a guy who had struck out twice in two at bats. That might be the thing they remembered, no matter what else I did. And another thing: you don't get all that much attention, not when there are a hundred guys in camp. They tend to work most with the bonus players, where they've got big money invested.

And then I said to myself: Who was to know the truth anyway? Maybe I would've struck out, no matter what, even if I'd had a full night's sleep. Maybe I was just making excuses for myself. There would be another game tomorrow, and who was to say I'd do any better? Lots of guys—most guys, in fact—who could rip sandlot pitching couldn't hit a lick in the minors.

I was walking back toward the barracks, feeling like an old, old man, when Mike called out to me.

"Hey, sonny," he yelled. (He'd picked that up from the sheriff and seemed to like the sound of it.) "Long distance call for you."

I took the call in the team office. It was from my father.

"Ted?" he said, his voice coming nearly two thousand miles down from New England, across the mountains and the snows, down the whole eastern seaboard into the warm Florida night. "How are you, son?"

"Fine, fine," I said, trying to sound cheerful.

"How are things going?"

"Great," I said.

"Are you playing a good game?" he asked.

"Just great," I said. "We had our first exhibition game today and I hit two over the fence."

One of the coaches, who was sitting there reading a baseball magazine, looked up at me. For one thing, there weren't any fences around the field; and for another, he knew darned well what I'd done today. Then he looked back to his magazine and pretended he wasn't listening.

"Did anybody else hit any over the fence?" my father asked.

"No," I said. "I was the only one. And I stole two bases."

Since I was telling lies I figured I might as well do a good job of it. My grandfather once said that untruths were like sausages—they come strung together. I'd never thought much about that until this moment. The longer you live the more you realize that your elders have lived too.

"I hit a double too," I said, adding another sausage.

The coach glanced up at me like he was in pain, as he flipped through the pages of the magazine.

"That's wonderful, Ted," my father said. "Keep up the good work. Everybody in town is asking about you, so I'll pass on the good word."

Then I spoke to my mother and kid brother. I slipped up and told my brother I'd hit two doubles. I hoped they wouldn't notice the difference. Sometimes those sausages can get tangled. Then I heard my father in the background saying this was costing money, and the goodbyes started.

As I was walking out of the office I heard the coach clearing his throat, the way you do when you want to say something without saying anything.

I felt really down when I walked outside. It wasn't that I hadn't ever lied to my father before; but all of a sudden there seemed to be a crucial difference between telling a lie and not wanting to tell the truth. What bugged me was the nature of the lie and the reasons for it. Why should I have been afraid to tell him that I'd had a bad day? Suppose I kept feeding him stories like that, and then at the end of two weeks got shipped home? I didn't know which I was afraid of more: my being proved wrong or his being proved right.

I went back out to the empty grandstand and sat

there again looking at the field. Beyond the trees that surrounded the outfield I could see the lights of the barracks and hear country music coming from transistors. Once in a while I'd hear somebody burst out in loud laughter. I guess those were the guys who had done okay today. Happiness has lots of sounds, while unhappiness is nothing but quiet.

· 6 ·

"EVERYBODY JUST STOPPED DEAD IN THEIR TRACKS," MIKE was saying. "And I mean everybody."

"Upshot too?" I asked excitedly.

"When I say everybody, I mean everybody. Listen, sonny, I was way out in the bullpen warming up and we stopped there too to watch it. It was just from the sound, the crack of the bat, that we knew. That sound carried a message. No mistake. I told the catcher, 'That's my buddy hit that ball.'"

"How about the people in the grandstands?" I asked. I couldn't help asking, I was so excited. We had a few dozen locals coming out each day to watch the action.

"They applauded," Mike said.

"And you say everybody took notice?"

"Say, I told you, didn't I? Look, sonny, it wasn't the moon landing or anything like that. It was just—"

It was just the longest ball I'd ever hit, that's all. And I knew even before I hit it that it was going to go. How can you explain it? It was my first time at bat in the game, and after yesterday's disaster I was determined to do something. The pitcher was throwing pellets up there, too. He'd fanned three of the first four men and was really challenging the hitters, throwing that fast one right in.

It was his second pitch to me. I'd taken one just to gauge his speed. He fired his second one right down my power alley—chest high on the inside—and the moment I saw it I knew it was going to go. I mean I really saw that ball. They say good hitters see more of the ball and I suddenly knew what that meant, because I saw that ball perfectly, full and round. And when you see it right your eyes don't let go of it until you get the bat on it.

I stepped into it and ripped it with everything I had. Then I took a few short steps down the line and raised my eyes to watch it go. That was unprofessional, I should have been hustling down the line; but I couldn't help it. It was a beautiful sight under any circumstances, and after yesterday even more so.

The right fielder trotted back and gave up. The ball carried clear over the palm trees in back of right field and kept going. I saw it bounce on the roof of the barracks and then jack-rabbit out of sight.

"Four hundred twenty feet," Mike said.

"Who said?" I asked.

We were sitting in the shade eating our lunch sandwiches and drinking from half-pint containers of milk. There was another game scheduled for the afternoon. Besides the big home run, I'd hit a double and a single and made a couple of good plays in the field, including a strong throw to get a runner at third.

"Pulski said," Mike said. "I heard him talking to one of the other managers."

"How'd he sound?" I asked, still so excited I could hardly swallow my chicken salad sandwich.

"Impressed, you dummy," Mike said, like he was getting impatient. "You think that big tub of spinach ever hit a ball that far? Now stop pumping yourself up—you'll probably go 0-for-four in the afternoon game."

But there was no chance of that, not the way I felt. I hit the ball so hard the first time up that I swear I must have flattened it on one side. It went for three bases to right center. The next time up I singled up the middle, and the last time (I was the only guy they left in to bat three times) I flied deep to center.

If feeling good at the plate is equal to hitting well, then that was the answer. I felt so strong and relaxed and confident that I think I could have hit with my eyes closed. And I knew exactly what was behind it all. Each time I stepped in I thought of my father. I made believe he was sitting in the grandstand watching me. Even as the pitcher wound up and delivered, and the ball came zipping down that invisible pipeline and busted in on me, I was thinking of my father. Even as I swung and made contact, he was right there, in my thoughts, and each time I started legging it down the line I was gritting my teeth in a sort of smile: I was going to prove it to him again and again that I was good, that I was going to be the best.

I felt as if I had some kind of secret weapon the other

guys didn't have: Prove it to the old man and make him proud.

Boy, you know you're going good when after the game the manager and some of the organization coaches walk over and talk to you. I'd seen them do that yesterday with a shortstop who'd shown a magic glove. A few of the top dogs walked over to him after the game and talked to him. It was no more than ten seconds and maybe all they said was "Good game, kid," but don't think every guy on the field didn't notice.

That's all they said to me. I was walking toward the barracks when Pulski and some of the others stopped me.

"Good hitting, Ted," Pulski said.

"Don't lose the stroke," another said.

"Yes sir," I said. Then I took off in a trot and headed for the shower, keeping my head down, trying to look real professional.

Spring training became one long stretch of joy after that. I was in real good shape now, loose and limber. I was hitting all kinds of pitching, righties and lefties. I swing lefty, but those lefthanders weren't giving me any trouble. I was digging in on them, determined not to be gun-shy, not even against the sidewheelers with the sweeping curve balls. If I couldn't pull them, then I went with the pitch and stroked my hits to left and left center. That's what the batting coach taught me.

Along with a few other guys who were ripping the ball, I was getting special attention from the batting coach—how not to overstride or overswing, to hold the bat steady, to wait on a pitch, things like that.

They had me playing center field, and there they taught me how to position myself, how to charge grounders, how to know which base to throw to, how to make sure I hit the cutoff man, and above all, how important it was to think ahead. You had to be alert to every possibility, so that whatever situation came up you'd be ready for it and know what you were going to do.

They had us in the sliding pit, too. You didn't just run and hit the dirt. You had to know how to slide, in order to avoid a tag and also so you wouldn't snap your ankle. One guy didn't know. He took a big leap into the pit, came down wrong and you could hear his ankle go. The poor guy was through for the year and maybe forever, because you never know how it's going to heal.

I called my father a couple of times (collect) to tell him how I was doing. He wasn't saying too much; after all, the fact that I had learned to hook slide was hardly the fulfillment of his dreams, but all the same, there was a nice, quiet pride in his voice when he told me to keep up the good work. I wanted to tell him that it was the thought of him that was driving me to do better than I ever thought I could, but somehow it didn't seem the thing to say.

My buddy Mike Delaney was also doing the job. In fact, he was showing as much smoke as any pitcher in camp. The pitching coaches were giving him the same kind of attention I was getting from the batting coach.

Mike really impressed me on the mound. He threw an overhand fast ball that hopped when it reached the batter like it was bouncing off some little nick in the air. And he had a great overhand curve that broke from the shoulders to the kneecaps. His problem was control, but they were working on him.

Then one day, after about ten days, they told the players to stick around after the game. The camp director, a wiry old-timer who'd played two years in the bigs about twenty years ago, started reading names from a list. You knew right off what it was all about, from the guys he was asking to hang around after the others had gone. There was the first baseman from Texas who couldn't hit, the left-hander from Cincinnati who couldn't find the plate, the catcher from Philly who couldn't run, the skinny pitcher from Richmond who'd been hit hard every time out.

He continued to call names. You never heard such a quiet group of guys. It was like listening to men being called out to be shot. Each name was like the tolling of a bell.

Suddenly I got scared. Some of the guys stepping out to form the second group had looked pretty good to me. One big guy, an outfielder from New York City, had hit some very long balls. But there he was, standing in the second group with his hands on his hips, staring down at the grass. You never could tell what the organization thought. If they thought you couldn't run or throw well enough, you were in trouble, since those were the God-given talents. You could teach a guy to hit or field, but those other things were either born into you or they weren't.

Suddenly I had the craziest thoughts. If my name was called, if they sent me home, I wouldn't go. I couldn't. I'd go to another camp and try out there, or I'd run away and get a job someplace. I wouldn't go home. What would I tell my father? What would everybody in town think? I could claim an injury. Pay some doctor five dollars to put a phony cast on my ankle and limp around town for a couple of weeks. That would be the best thing. Everybody would understand, and I'd get sympathy, and my father wouldn't have to be ashamed because his son had failed.

But then it was over. The director folded up his sheet of paper and put it into his hip pocket.

"The rest of you fellows," he said with an energy that hadn't been in his voice when he was reading the names, "hit the showers."

I walked away slowly, head down, trying not to look at the group staying behind. There were a good twenty-five or thirty guys there. Each had been a star in his home town, each had brought his hopes and his dreams south with him. I felt sorry for them, standing out there in the sunshine. But at the same time I felt a little bigger than I had before. You can't help feeling that. It's not that you're glad for somebody else's misfortune, it's just that you've got a feeling of achievement, or pride, or something, knowing that you went into the competition and came out—so far, anyway—ahead.

I heard the beginning of what the camp director said.

"Boys," he started, "this is the saddest part of spring training. Not everybody can make a club. Now, we can make mistakes too . . ."

That's all I heard. Somehow even hearing that much made me feel guilty. I took off at a trot for the showers.

You never heard such a loud, noisy shower room. We were singing and yelling. It was all that bottled-up fear coming out, I guess. We'd known cut-down day was coming, and we were the survivors.

Dinner was quiet, though. Right off, the guys who were going home banded together at certain tables, talking quietly among themselves. Guys who had hardly known each other before were now friends, for a little while anyway. Occasionally I stole a glance at them, wondering what they were thinking, what they were going to tell the people back home.

The rest of us talked quietly too, as if out of respect for the other fellows. It was tough keeping quiet, what with all the excitement we were feeling, but maybe it was because we knew we were truly professionals now that we were able to conduct ourselves so as not to make the others feel bad.

After dinner I went with Mike to place calls home. My father wasn't so excited about the big news. I guess he'd come to expect it, after all the good reports I'd been giving. And another thing was, failure was something my father didn't believe in. I guess it had never come into his head that I might not make it. If only he could've seen some of those back-breaking curves I'd had to hit!

He congratulated me and promised that sometime during the season they would come and visit. That was about it. Then I went outside and waited while Mike made his call.

When he came out about five minutes later, Mike had a soft smile on his face.

"He cried when I told him," he said.

"Who cried?" I asked.

"My father. I could hear it in his voice. I said, 'What's the matter, Pop?' And he said, 'I'm crying, I'm so happy. That's all.'"

"That's nice," I said. I guess I was a little bit envious. Mike's father was a real ball fan. "He really wants you to make it, huh?" I asked as we headed into town for a soda.

"Sure, man. Doesn't yours?"

"Well," I said, "he wants to see me make it, sure; but he's not much of a ball fan."

"How come?"

"I don't know," I said impatiently. I didn't want to talk about it.

As we walked under the trees and the Main Street lights came into view, Mike said, "So we're in."

We were going to be sent to Wyattville, a class D club in Virginia, after spring training—another ten days or so.

"Yeah," I said. I felt tired. I hoped it rained tomorrow. I wanted a day off just to think about everything.

Suddenly Mike stopped in the middle of the street, threw his arms up into the air, and yelled out to the Florida night: "We're going to be Big Leaguers!"

· 7 ·

WE BROKE CAMP NEAR THE END OF APRIL ON A RAINY DAY
with the wind blowing through the palm trees and the
rain beating against the windows of the barracks. The
place had seemed smaller after cut-down date, after thirty
guys had left. And quieter, too. There was less horseplay
and fooling around; everybody had become more serious
about things.

We packed our bags while the rain was beating down.
Then, because we were three teams splitting up to go off
in our separate directions, there were lots of goodbyes
and wishes for good luck. The last ten or fifteen minutes
or so, while we were waiting to be called to the buses,
were very quiet. The guys were sitting on their cots or
standing looking out of the windows at the rain, each one
alone with his thoughts. I guess you might say we were
like soldiers finished with basic training, heading out
now for the real thing.

Standing at the window, I could see the diamonds.
Rain falling on an empty ball field is a sad thing to see.

We headed north on the team bus, a rattly old boiler-
maker that couldn't do more than forty miles an hour

and barely made it up steep hills. But it had a new coat of paint and the team name in big letters on the side, and as we cruised north up through Florida and Georgia people looked at it and wondered who we were.

We stopped off in central Georgia to play an exhibition game with Seltonia, the organization's class B club. This was a team made up mostly of second-year men. We hadn't seen them in Florida because they had been working out in another town.

Well, we were feeling pretty cocky about ourselves when we got out on the field. After all, we were a team of brand-new professionals. But then we had a look at their starting pitcher. He was warming up down the right field line and the sight of him turned us cold. He was a right-hander with a big kick and he was firing that ball so that you could hear it all over the park going like a pistol shot into the catcher's glove.

They trimmed us 13-1. Mike did best against them, giving up only two runs in the three innings he worked. He was amazed. "They don't swing at bad pitches," he told me later. They didn't throw many either. We managed only three hits. I got one of them, out-running the third baseman's peg on a dinker down the line that I barely got around on.

It was a most discouraging experience. Here these other guys were only in a B league and they had made us look like semipros. What was it like on top? It seemed light years away, a whole other world, inhabited by supermen.

So we went on to Wyattville, and it was a very quiet trip.

I was used to small towns, so Wyattville looked pretty usual to me. But for some of the guys from places like Chicago, Indianapolis, and Baltimore, it was a real shocker.

"We're gonna live here for the next five months?"— was the general feeling, spoken with dismay.

Well, I guess Wyattville was kind of small, by any standards. It was in southwestern Virginia, tucked away in the Blue Ridge Mountains. There was a main street five blocks long, one movie house (it opened at seven o'clock and had only one show), a couple of restaurants and luncheonettes, a pool hall, a hotel, and not much more.

We came rolling in at eight o'clock on a Monday morning. The season was opening the next night, at home. I think the guys were expecting some sort of welcome from the town, a band or a cheering section or something. After all, we were there to uphold the honor of Wyattville in the South Virginia League. But there was nothing. A few people stopped on the sidewalk to stare curiously at us; and one old man with a face like a walnut who looked like he was hobbling on sore feet, cupped his hands around his mouth and yelled, "Play ball!" and laughed to himself like he'd made the greatest joke in the world.

We went straight to the ball park to stow our gear. The field was about a mile outside of town. As we filed through the gate, past the empty ticket-taker's booth, we went out to have a look at the field. Well, it was something less than major league. There were small grandstands behind first and third. The light towers looked kind of skimpy. The grass needed cutting, especially in the outfield. The outfield fence was made of wooden planks about ten feet high and looked like a well-hit ball would go right through it. At one spot in left center it was covered with a blanket.

"Why is that blanket there?" Pulski asked the grounds-keeper, a little old man who wore an ancient baseball cap with white stripes on it.

"Most of the planks have fallen out," the old man said. "There's a big hole there."

"Fix it by tomorrow night."

"Surely," the old man said.

"I have some boys who charge the fences. I don't want them disappearing," Pulski said. He was a bit miffed, we could tell. He'd seen better-looking fields in his day, I guess. Then he asked the old man to trim the grass, get the broken glass out of the outfield, and lay down the foul lines.

The clubhouse was another disappointment. It was a squared-off concrete building behind the first base grandstand. All it was, really, was a room with whitewashed walls and a concrete floor and roof. There were wooden benches along the walls and over them were the "lockers" —big metal hooks on which to hang your gear. There was one shower and a stall john and a desk in the far corner for Pulski. That was it. Welcome to professional baseball. I'd read about big league clubhouses: wall-to-wall carpeting, enormous steel lockers, a dozen showers with tile floors, comfortable chairs, television, soda machines.

"Think there's water in the shower?" Mike asked.

"You'll probably be the first one to find out," I said. Pulski had told him he was starting the opening game.

"My high school locker room looked better," said Walt Casey, our first baseman.

"The difference here," Neil Edgerly, a pitcher, said, "is that you're getting paid."

"Take it as it comes, chums," said Herb Markson, the skinny shortstop.

"The best way to get out of here is hit," Bill Gruber, an outfielder, said.

"Or not hit!" somebody else said. There's always one gloomy guy.

Later, we went back to town and assembled in the team office, which was located over a restaurant on Main Street. There we were introduced to the business manager, a local named Spider McCann. He was a friendly guy, bald-headed, with a bright smile and a belly that hung out and covered his belt. He shook hands with all eighteen of us, said to each guy, "Glad to see yuh," and wished us luck.

The first order of business was to get us located. Spider had a list of private homes around town that rented rooms to ballplayers. He said the prices were all pretty much the same. The only guy who decided to stay in the hotel was the only guy who could afford it, Jesse Nolan, who had signed for a bonus of thirty thousand. He even had a car, and had got permission to drive up from Florida. Mike buttered him up a lot during spring training because he was hoping to borrow the car during the season, though where he'd go with it in that part of the country, I didn't know.

Mike and I were rooming together, naturally, so we hiked off to one of the houses which was a short walk from the ballpark to rent our room.

Well, you don't get rich playing minor league ball. We were getting four hundred a month, and out of that had to pay all our expenses. It said in the contract that the club paid your expenses on the road, but since we always came back to Wyattville after a road game—and some of those other towns were as much as seventy-five miles away—the team really didn't spring for anything, outside of buying you a few hot dogs between games of a doubleheader when you were on the road.

The house was a nicely kept two story place, with a front porch and a back yard, surrounded by shade trees. Mr. and Mrs. Harrison, the owners, were letting an upstairs bedroom, once slept in by their children, who were now grown and living elsewhere. We took the room, then called Spider and asked him to drive over with our suitcases when he had the time, as he had promised he would do for all the guys.

Then we hiked back to the business office, left our

address and phone number with Spider, and went downstairs to the restaurant to have some lunch. The owner of the place, Watson, recognized us right away as ballplayers and came over and shook our hands.

"Pizza on the house for the whole team every time somebody hits a home run," he said.

"He's going to make you go broke," Mike told him, pointing to me.

"Most anybody's ever hit for the club is nineteen," Watson said.

"My boy'll have that inside the first month," Mike said.

Watson laughed politely. I guess he'd seen lots of young ballplayers passing through Wyattville, and no doubt every one had been proud and ambitious and confident.

"We'll see," he said.

"We'll be in for pizza tomorrow night, after the game," I said.

· 8 ·

NOW THAT WAS THE DUMBEST THING I EVER SAID IN MY life. There I was, not in town more than a few hours, talking to this fellow who was trying to be friendly, and shooting off my mouth like that. Nobody could predict that he was going to hit a home run. You might get four hits, but no home runs. You could hit long blasts and see them die in the wind. You might get a couple of walks, and otherwise not see a decent pitch to swing at. A hundred things could happen. Never, never say you're going to hit a home run.

But what do you do after you've said it?

It wasn't as if I wasn't nervous enough, playing my first game of professional baseball. The lights were on and the grandstands were filled even though it was a chilly night. Maybe because it was the first game ever for me, but everything looked beautiful. The grass had been trimmed and was a bright green under the lights, the ball looked whiter than any ball I had ever seen and seemed to be flashing through the air.

They announced the starting lineups over the PA system and for the first time I heard my name in a booming, unreal voice: *"Batting fourth, Ted Marshall, center field."* Then they played the national anthem, and there I was, in professional baseball.

I can tell you just what it felt like as I stood out in center field waiting for the first pitch to be thrown. I felt as if I was in the big leagues, starring in a world series, on television, with seventy-five million people watching. I felt older, as if I had a whole history of success behind me. I felt I could jump thirty feet in the air to make a catch, if I had to. All of center field seemed no bigger than a postage stamp. Feeling, actually feeling speed in your body is an unbelievably beautiful sensation.

Mike threw his fast ball past the first two men. The third guy hit to short where Herb Markson fumbled. The next man popped to short and that was it. And it was for the history books, because in pro ball they keep records of everything and it stays there forever.

I came up in the bottom of the first with a man on second and two out. The other pitcher, a chunky right-hander with a medium fast ball and a good curve, stood out there sizing me up. I was staring back at him, the bat on my shoulder, waiting for him to start his motion. All of a sudden I had a confusion of thoughts, about my first time up in professional baseball, about my father, and about Watson and his pizza pies.

I took the first pitch, even though it was a good one, belt high and over the plate. I just had to have a clean look at the first pitch thrown to me in pro ball, even though I knew it was going to be a strike against me.

Then I set myself, cocking the bat back behind my left ear, bent slightly at the waist, my eyes on the ball in the pitcher's hand. That's all I watched, not his face or his motion or his kick. He leaned back out of his stretch, kicked and threw. The ball came zipping in, another fast ball, maybe a trifle outside, but no matter. I stepped into it, timed it perfectly and got good wood on it. I pulled it into the right center alley and took off. I cut first base and kept going. The center fielder was just running it down as I came into second and saw Pulski waving me on from the third base coaching box. I came into third standing up.

There was nice applause and while I stood on third with my hands on my hips, panting, I saw Mike stand up in our little wooden dugout and yell,

"Way to go, Teddy!"

By the time I came up for the last time in the eighth we were ahead 7-1. Mike was pitching like a machine. In my other times at bat I'd walked, lined to second, and singled. As I stepped into the box I really set my sights on that fence. Nobody had hit one out. I knew the dumbest thing you could do was go for a home run. It throws off your timing and everything. You're just supposed to swing hard and try to meet the ball. If it goes, it goes. If you have the power you'll get your share.

But my big mouth had put me on the spot. And the pitcher was a lefty now, no less. He was a stringbean of a guy with a good snapping curve. He threw me two curves, for a ball and a strike, and now I guessed fast ball (another dumb thing—you're not supposed to guess).

And he threw the fast one, right into my wheelhouse, and I really whacked it. I watched it soar off, rising and rising into the night. As I trotted down the line all the guys jumped up and yelled, "Pizza!" I saw the right-fielder standing with his back to the plate and his hands on his hips, looking up.

There is nothing more elegant than the home-run trot.

After eating the pizza (and getting slapped on the back by everybody, including Upshot), I decided to call my father. It was almost midnight, but I figured he wouldn't mind.

When he heard my voice he asked if anything was the matter.

"I hit a single, triple, and home run tonight," I yelled into the phone. Some of the guys still hanging around Watson's heard me and broke into mock applause.

"That's very nice, Ted," my father said.

"I won pizza for the whole team with the home run."

"Pizza?" he asked. I remembered now that he hated the stuff.

"They give a free one if you hit a home run," I said.

"Don't eat too much of it," he said.

"I hope I eat one every night."

"Are you all right?" he asked. "Do you need any money?"

"No, I'm fine. I've got enough money."

"Listen, I'm glad you had a good game, but next time call earlier, okay?"

"Did I wake you?"

"No, but you might have."

I said goodbye, then hung up.

"What'd he say?" Mike asked me as we walked home.

"He said not to eat too much pizza," I said.

"Well, he was joking, wasn't he?"

"He doesn't joke."

The streets were absolutely quiet, not a person, not a car, not a sound. All around us the mountains rose in total darkness. There wasn't a light on in any house.

"He doesn't understand," I said.

"Not everybody's a baseball fan," Mike said.

"That's not it. He doesn't understand what I feel. That's what bugs me."

"He'll come around, you'll see."

"I think even if I hit .400, he still wouldn't dig it. I don't mean the .400, but what it means to me."

"He'll get the message sooner or later. Anyway, it seems to me you worry too much what he thinks."

"No I don't."

"Sure you do."

"Hey, I said I don't."

He shrugged. "If you say so."

But he was right, I did. And it was foolish. So he wasn't a baseball fan. No, that wasn't it. He just didn't care about what I cared about. But I knew how to change that, because I knew what impressed him. Maybe he didn't understand what .400 meant, but he certainly understood success. That's what baseball was about. That's what everything was about.

· 9 ·

WELL, AFTER WE WON THAT FIRST GAME WE DROPPED THE next three. We didn't win another until Mike pitched again. The problem was, the team wasn't looking so good. The infield was leaky, the other pitchers were getting racked up, and we lacked punch in the lineup.

After two weeks we were in last place. Upshot put us through some afternoon workouts, but it didn't help. We kept losing. After three weeks we'd won six and lost fourteen. The big team in the league was Mt. Carleton; they were off streaking, winning sixteen of their first nineteen. They had muscles in the lineup and pitchers that made the air blister.

After the third week Upshot released Walt Casey the first baseman and one of the pitchers, who had an ERA like the national debt. That scared the guys and we played a little better, but only a little. The new first baseman, Charley Garelli, hit better than Walt and won a few games for us, but we were still dragging last in the six-team league.

But how bad can you feel when you're hitting .360? I couldn't help not sharing in the general gloom. Somebody had told me in spring training that in the minors you don't find the team effort that you do in the majors. It's every man for himself, because you're competing with one another for promotion to the next team up the ladder. Only so many can go up and each guy wants it to be him. That's not the way it should be, but that's the way it is. You don't actually root against a teammate, but you do root entirely for yourself.

The team got a lot of kidding from the local people, but it was in a good-natured way because they felt sorry for us. Because we were going so good—or maybe it was because everybody else was going so bad—Mike and I were getting a lot of attention. The Wyattville paper printed feature stories about us and we were invited to sit in for a free lunch with the local Kiwanis club. Of our six wins, Mike had five. He even beat Mt. Carleton once.

Morale can go only so low, I guess, and then it starts to pick up. Once we realized we weren't going to win the pennant, everybody sort of accepted our "condition," as Upshot called it one night. There was a lot of joking among ourselves about how lousy we were (never when the skipper was around, though).

But there is nothing as silent as the bus ride home after dropping a game on the road. Even if you feel like loosening up a little, you can't, because the manager is sitting there. Attitude in a young ballplayer is important, and fooling around after losing shows a bad attitude and can be marked against you. Those rides home, sometimes two hours through an absolutely pitch black country night, were really dismal. There were a couple of clubs that didn't have showers for the visiting teams and after those games we rode home in our sweaty uniforms, and no matter how chilly the night, we kept all windows open.

After about a third of the season had gone by, I was still going strong. My average stayed between .340 and .360 and I was hitting all kinds of pitching. In addition, I'd earned the team eleven pizzas so far with the long ball, and Watson the restaurant man was beginning to shake his head about his generosity. He told Spider one day, "I would have done better this year to give a pie for every game they won instead of for every homer." He wasn't far wrong either.

I got a surprise one day when I called home. My father was out and my mother took the call.

"We're all so proud, Ted," she said. (I'd been sending home the newspaper clippings.) "You should see your father. He carries those clippings with him wherever he goes and tells everyone how well you're doing."

"He does?" I asked.

"He talks batting average instead of stock market."

"He does?" I asked again.

"At the last Chamber of Commerce meeting he read aloud one of the newspaper stories, the one about how fast you run and how swift you throw."

"I didn't think he was following it that carefully," I said.

"Of course he is," she said. "He's very proud. Somebody stopped him in the street yesterday and asked what you were batting. 'Three fifty-six,' he said." She laughed. "I never thought I'd see the day."

Neither did I. It was really a surprise to me. Whenever we talked he was as stiff as ever when it came to how I was doing. Maybe he was feeling embarrassed now, since he had been so against it in the beginning. I'd proved that I had been right and he had been wrong. But still, you don't like to think about your father that way. There was nobody who wished better for me, I knew that. But why the devil couldn't he yell into the phone "Great!" the way Mike's father did? You didn't have to be a baseball fan to know how to make a guy feel good.

"He's a front runner," Mike said that night as we sat on the porch of our house. We'd lost another game, so there was nothing new to talk about.

"What do you mean?" I asked.

"Your old man's a front runner. You're doing good so he wants to climb on the bandwagon and share in the glory."

"That's not true," I said. "That's a lousy thing to say."

"Yeah?" he asked. He'd taken to smoking cigars now with his success, and he had a big one rammed between his teeth, blowing clouds of smoke into the quiet night air.

"He's been rooting for me from the start."

"Yeah?" he said again, and with that cigar he looked like a real wise guy.

"Yeah," I said.

Now he took the cigar out of his mouth and leaned toward me.

"Sonny," he said, "suppose you were hitting .220, like the rest of the great stickmen on this club."

"He'd still be with me, giving me encouragement," I said.

He put the cigar back into his mouth and said, "Yeah?"

"You don't think he'd be glad, do you?"

"Don't ask me," he said. "I don't know the man."

Who does? I thought glumly.

·10·

It was a woman that caused the downfall of Mike Delaney.

It happened around the middle of June when, except for the fact that the team was losing so many games that a game postponed by rain was looked upon as a victory of sorts, everything was going well. From the selfish point of view, that is. I was still hitting a ton, in fact I was second in the league in batting, and Mike was having a fine year. He was leading the league in strikeouts, and so was Herb Markson: the difference was that Mike was a pitcher and Herb was a shortstop.

We first noticed the two girls when we were sitting in Watson's one afternoon. We were in a booth having breakfast and they were at the counter having sodas.

"They're talking about us," I said to Mike.

"Who?" he asked.

"Those two at the counter."

I could tell they were from the way they'd sneak looks at us and then right away whisper something to the other behind their hands, then giggle.

Mike looked at them from the corner of his eye, sort

of sizing them up. He had a very stern look on his face, the way he never looked except when standing on the mound trying to stare down a hitter. He was trying to be mature about this. When girls giggle, you don't; when they don't, then you have to make the laughs. That lesson in the art of romance was preached to me by Michael Delaney, who claimed he had a girlfriend back home, though they had "agreed not to write letters to each other because it was too sad." That was his story.

"Not bad," he muttered after studying the girls.

"You mean, pretty good," I said.

Mine was a blonde. I say "mine" because right off you sense how it's going to be. Any time two couples are going to be matched off even a stranger can tell which way it's going to be. The blonde had long hair that hung down below her shoulders. She had a way of peeking her half glances at us that suggested mischief; like her eyes were smiling. The brunette, Mike's girl, was bolder. Sometimes she'd spin right around on her stool and look at us, smiling a smile that was more like laughing. She was cute but not as cute as the blonde. The blonde was slim, while the brunette was kind of round. The blonde was built like a shortstop, while the brunette looked more like a catcher. What better way to describe them?

So we continued to sit in the booth like a couple of dummies while those girls kept peeking and giggling and spinning on their stools. They weren't going to do that forever, I knew. Sooner or later they'd give up and leave. I kept looking at Mike and he kept looking at me, each pretending we weren't interested but wouldn't mind if the other made a move.

Then the brunette broke the ice, so to speak. All of a sudden she said, right out loud (the restaurant was empty), "My father says Mike Delaney is the best pitcher Wyattville's had in five years."

Then she tilted her head to the side and stared at Mike with pure mischief.

Without a word, he got up and walked between the tables to her. He held out his hand and said, "Thank your father and give him this for me." They shook hands. Then he took everybody by surprise, most especially the brunette, and leaned forward and kissed her on the cheek. "And that's for you," he said.

The blonde's name was Susannah, she was seventeen, lived in Wyattville with her family, her father was a garage mechanic, and she wanted to be a teacher. She liked picnics, country music, and baseball. Baseball? She swore it was true. How many games had she seen this season? None, yet, she confessed, but she was not going to miss another home game, she promised.

She said she loved baseball ever since her older brother tried out for the team at the University of Virginia, and she still loved it even though her brother didn't make it. I asked Spider to give me a pass for her and he tore a blank sheet of paper off his writing pad, handed it to me and said this and seventy-five cents would get her into the ball park. Big joke. So I asked Pulski to take her in with him and old Upshot came through. And this is what he said, with a little smile: "It's a different world for .350 hitters."

The brunette's name was Catherine, and Mike called her The Great, after a certain figure in history. She lived in town with her family, same as Susannah. Her father was in real estate, she wanted to be a teacher too, and she also claimed to love baseball, even though she'd never seen a game. Upshot got her through the gate too. And this is what he told Mike: "A star pitcher should have a girlfriend. It lends him dignity, as long as he doesn't break curfew."

Upshot had adjusted himself to a losing team. Mike said it was a big man who could make jokes in the face of defeat.

"Defeat?" I said. "What's that?"

I guess I was feeling pretty big those days. A .350 batting average, a good all-round game, and Susannah. Things were going better for me than I had ever dreamed they could.

One night I had dinner at Susannah's house and told her father I'd surely be in the big leagues inside of three years, maybe less. He gave me a big smile and looked real impressed.

"We'd be mighty proud of you, Ted, if you did that," he said.

Later, while we were having coffee, the phone rang. Susannah's father answered it and I heard him say,

"Can't talk now; got Ted Marshall here for dinner."

He sounded real pleased to be saying it. People like to be close to somebody who's making a success. So I just sat back and told them what life was like in the big leagues. After all, I'd read about it in the baseball magazines.

One day Cappy Donovan, the director of the big team's whole minor league system, stopped off in Wyattville. He did that every summer, swinging through all the minor league towns for a day or two to size up the players. We knew he was there and everybody was trying their best. I had a pretty good game, getting three singles. I tried to hit one out the last time up, to get him a piece of free pizza, but struck out.

"You looked bad the last time up," he said to me later. We were sitting upstairs in the team's office, just him and me.

"Well, I did okay the other times," I said.

"That doesn't count," he said.

He was middle-aged, gray haired, with a tough, lined face that had seen a lot of weather. He was wearing a short-sleeved shirt and had powerful arms, like a weightlifter's. He stared at me a lot, like he was trying to size me up on the inside. When he wasn't talking he chewed on his bottom lip.

"You were trying to hit it out, weren't you?" he asked.

"Sort of," I said, and felt like I was making a confession.

"You can try that once in a while, when your club needs a run, but never against the kind of pitches you saw."

I'll tell you what I saw—low sweepers that were away from me, thrown by a lefthander who knew what he was doing.

"The pitch you struck out on was out of the strike zone."

Boy, he was really watching. It wasn't *that* far out.

"Pulski says you swing at too many bad pitches."

"But I get hits."

"Not for long. You'll start going for worse pitches. Before you know it the pitchers will be rolling it up and you'll be swinging at it."

"Yes sir," I said.

"And you were sloppy in the field."

"I was?" I wondered how. I'd made four putouts and didn't mishandle anything.

"Once you ran the left fielder off a ball when you shouldn't have."

"Center field's supposed to grab whatever he can."

"But he's not supposed to play as if he's alone out there. Also, you charged a grounder like a maniac."

"We were taught that in spring training," I said.

"You were taught to come in like that when you have to make a throw or if there's a danger of a man taking an extra base on the hit. The man who hit that ball, if you noticed, was heavy set; he was no threat to try and make second. You took an unnecessary chance. The ball goes through and even that fat boy makes it to third."

Then he stopped talking (for which I was grateful) and stared at me for almost a minute, chewing on that bottom lip like it was taffy.

"Nevertheless," he said, "you're playing good ball. We want you to keep improving, that's all."

"My swing okay?" I asked. I wanted to hear *something* good.

"Your swing is fine. Stay the way you are. Don't let those lefties back you off."

"They don't scare me," I said. I had the sore ribs to prove it.

"That's right," he said. Then he said, real mean, "Remember: you're better than they are. Just keep that in your head and you'll play winning ball. And that's the name of this game: win. Some of you young fellows think you're still in high school and are just having some fun out there. But this is professional ball and you're expected to do well and win. It's no different from any other vocation. There's winning and nothing else."

He sounded more than mean now; he sounded almost fanatic about it. I was going to mention that when somebody wins it means somebody else has to lose. But I didn't think he'd want to hear that.

·11·

"YOU'RE GOING UP," MIKE SAID. "I'VE GOT THE FEELING."

"You mean to Seltonia?"

Seltonia, Pennsylvania, was the B club—the one that had slaughtered us in Georgia.

"I'll bet," Mike said.

"How can you know?"

"He talked to you, didn't he? He didn't talk to anybody else, did he? Not even me. I know they won't move me up this year; I'm still too wild. But I'll bet they jump you."

I couldn't believe it. In some ways I didn't want it. I would have hated to leave Mike, and Susannah, too, of course. But if they jump you in mid-year it really means something. Then if I went up and kept hitting in B, why, I might even get to go to camp with the big team next spring.

"Seltonia needs some more hitting in their outfield," Mike said.

That was true. We followed them in *The Sporting News*. We followed the whole organization, right up to the top. We knew what everybody was doing. Every ballplayer does that. It's like you're waiting for somebody to die or something.

Cappy had moved on now, leaving behind a state of depression. He'd seen two games and we lost both. It's bad enough to be losing, but worse when the front office is there. Even Jesse Nolan, our bonus baby, was doing poorly. He was hitting a grim .205, but they had him playing every day all the same. When the team has big money tied up in you they don't give up that easily. Of the original eighteen men that had come north, six had already been released. The new guys weren't doing much better. Losing can be contagious, I think.

We were sitting in the little playground behind the public school, waiting for the girls. We hadn't seen them the past two nights because Cappy was in town. Trying to make a good impression, we'd gone straight home after eating, getting in way before curfew. It was the first time that we were in so early.

"The team owes us some time," Mike said. "We ought to break it tonight."

"I'm not so sure."

"Listen, even if you get caught, so you get fined five bucks. So what?"

"It's not the money," I said. "They just don't like you doing it. It goes on your record."

Pulski sent in a report on every player after every game. I don't know if he reported night-owling or not, but I didn't want it down against me.

"The stars of the team ought to have privileges," Mike said.

"We've got enough."

We sure did. We were always being invited out to dinner, the manager of the movie theater let us in for nothing, and the town department store gave us twenty-five dollars worth of free merchandise each just for hanging around the store one afternoon talking to people. Spider McCann called us "The Swaggerers," because he said we walked different from the rest of the team. When you've got a status, you've got to live up to it, is what I say.

The game had ended at 10:30. We'd showered, dressed, and eaten in a hurry, so there was plenty of time. We told the girls to meet us in the playground at 11:30.

The school was just outside of town, and there weren't any houses around, so it was a good place to fool around and make noise, if you felt like it. The playground was grass covered and had swings and a sliding pond and climbing bars and the strangest little contraption: a wooden merry-go-round that you pushed by hand. It had small wooden seats, each with a railing to hang on to. If you kept throwing the thing around you could get it going pretty fast, since it was for small children and wasn't very big.

The girls finally showed up, each with a bag of popcorn.

We walked over to the swings and sat there eating the popcorn, lined up on the swings. It doesn't sound like much, but those were very happy times. There we were, Mike and me, two ballplayers doing what we loved and doing it well, sitting with two girls we really liked, out in the mild and quiet night, just sitting on children's swings eating popcorn and listening to the warm mountain breeze going *shhhhh* through the trees.

I hadn't told my father about Susannah, nor my mother neither. But him especially. I don't know why. There wasn't much communication at all. I called home once or twice a week, sent them the clippings, wrote a letter, and that was it. The last time we'd spoken he asked if I was still enjoying it. The question almost floored me. The idea of *not* enjoying baseball was so far from my mind it could have been the furthest, tiniest star in the universe. And anyway, what could have given him the notion that I might stop enjoying it? It wasn't the kind of thing you turned on and off. Did I ever ask him if he still enjoyed being a lawyer?

"Are you enjoying the popcorn?" Mike asked me all of a sudden, real sly. I was going to have to stop telling him everything. He was getting too frisky.

"Bottle it," I said.

"Are you enjoying the swing?" he asked now.

"Are you enjoying your insanity?" I asked him.

"He's not insane," Cathy the Great said. She was loyal.

"All pitchers are insane," I said. "Or if not, then they become that way. It comes from all the winding up they do, from swinging their arms back the way they do. Doctors say it loosens all the muscles from the shoulders on up and makes things sag inside the head. It's a fact."

"It is not," The Great said. But I think she half believed it.

"Well, you'd better watch him carefully all the same," I said.

Then I felt Susannah's hand on my arm. I looked at her and she was smiling at me, her head tilted slightly to a side. It was not a smile that said or meant anything. It was just a smile. We stared at each other for not more than five seconds, though in heart-time it was closer to five years, and when it finally got up into memory, it seemed a lifetime.

"Let's ride the merry," Mike said.

The girls were afraid and we had to coax them, promising not to push it too fast. We promised and they believed.

They sat down on the small wooden seats and held on to the rails. I stood at one side of the thing and Mike at the other. We began pushing it, giving it a shove each time one of the seats came circling by. We started shoving harder and harder. The thing began picking up speed. The seats and the railings and the girls were coming around faster and faster.

Now the girls started yelling for us to stop, but there wasn't a chance of that happening. I watched Mike on the other side and he had this big foolish grin on his face, and I saw him buck each time he gave the thing another shove. The old wooden merry-go-round was groaning and grunting and probably moving faster than ever before in its history. The girls kept whirling around, kept yelling. The wind was tearing through Susannah's long blonde hair and making it fly.

Finally I got tired and sat down on the grass, but Mike kept it going another few minutes, and the girls continued flashing by with their yelling and their flying hair. Then Mike let the thing go on its own and sat down on the grass. We watched the rocky old turn-around start to slow down. The girls weren't coming around so fast as they had. Finally it stopped and they sat there in the little seats shaking their heads and panting.

"Never again," Susannah said. "I'm never getting on again."

"It's fun," Mike said.

Susannah was so dizzy I had to help her off. Cathy the Great said she wanted to sit absolutely still for at least five minutes, that while the merry-go-round had stopped her stomach was still moving. She gave Mike a dirty look.

"It's all in fun," he said.

I was going to hear those words inside my head all winter. And when I wasn't thinking them I was re-minded of them whenever Mike wrote me a letter from his snowed-in little town in the Midwest. "Keep away from the fun," he wrote. "Look out for the fun."

·12·

"M_Y ARM HURTS," MIKE SAID.

It was the following morning. We were lying in our beds, the sunlight flooding through the screened windows.

"I'm not surprised," I said. "That was like pitching nine innings, pushing that thing the way you did."

"Well," he said, "I've got another nine to go tonight."

He didn't say anything more about his arm that day, though a few times I saw him wheel it around slowly. Most pitchers are pretty crazy when it comes to their arms. The least twinge gives them worry. I know some who won't even use their pitching arm for a handshake. So I didn't give Mike's complaint any further thought, especially since he didn't mention it again.

That night he suffered his earliest kayo of the season —one and one-third innings. To me, standing out in center field watching him, he didn't seem to be working with his usual smooth delivery. He was a nice pitcher to watch, coming over the top with most of his pitches, throwing with what seemed little effort. But tonight he seemed to be pushing the ball, like he was tight in the shoulder.

• 82 •

"Feel okay?" I asked him after the game.

"Wounded pride, that's all," he said with a little grin that seemed forced.

He was pretty quiet the next couple of days. In fact, one afternoon I didn't see him at all. When he showed up just in time to catch the bus for a road game and I asked him where he'd been, he said, "Walkin'."

He started that night against Mt. Carleton. Granted, they were the hardest hitters in the league, but the way they tore into him was unbelievable. I had balls hit over my head that took off like golf shots. Mike was taken out in the third.

The bus ride back that night was its usual quiet self after a loser. But even after losers Mike and I always found something to say. We'd usually sit in the back and talk quietly about the girls. But tonight there wasn't a word said. He sat at the window, biting on his thumb nail and watching the night go by. It was a ninety minute ride, and not one word out of him.

When we were walking home I finally said,

"Okay, what is it?"

"What's what?" he asked.

"You know. What's bugging you?"

"Nothing."

"Nothing, huh?"

"Mind your business, Ted."

So I didn't push it.

The next afternoon we borrowed Jesse Nolan's car and took the girls for a ride down the highway. We bought a picnic lunch at a roadside place, pitched a blanket in an open field, and ate. There was none of the usual horseplay. Mike sat quietly most of the time, staring off at the mountains. When he did say something, did crack a joke, it had a pretty sharp bite to it.

"What's wrong with him?" Susannah asked me as we took a walk off by ourselves.

"Nothing," I said.

"Cathy feels he doesn't like her anymore."

"He's out with her, isn't he?" I asked.

"But he's not talking to her."

"He's not talking to anybody."

"But why?"

"Look, he's been creamed his last two times out," I said. "He's not used to it."

"Oh, is that it?"

"Naturally." Here I was, telling her an untruth and getting sore because she didn't seem to understand the seriousness of it.

"That's what makes baseball such a crazy game," she said. "One day you're good and the next day you're bad. It doesn't make sense."

It made perfect sense, and it was what made baseball such a great game. You had to work hard every day in order to have a good game, and nobody gave anything for free. But there's only so much you can explain to an outsider.

On the drive home Mike suddenly got into good humor again. He started singing some country songs, putting a crazy Irish brogue to the words and we laughed all the way home.

"Haven't been loose lately," he said as we walked to the ball park for that night's game.

"How do you feel now?" I asked.

"Great, great," he said.

In the dugout before the game Upshot walked over to him and said,

"Can you give me a few innings tonight if I need you?"

"Sure," Mike said.

Well, it was one of those games. Leo Corbett, our starter, got shelled in the first, and by the fourth we were down 8–1. Then we started hitting, and by the seventh it was 10–7, with us still on the down side. But then I came up with two on and put one on a line out to dead center. It was as good a ball as I'd hit all season and it had just enough rise to clear the fence. The few hundred people in the stands gave me a big hand and as I trotted home I noticed Mike warming up down in the pen.

Upshot was all excited, walking back and forth in the dugout slamming his big hands together, saying that this was a big one and let's hold them. It would have been a good game to win, coming from so far behind and all, and the club felt real good, especially with our best pitcher coming in. Ordinarily, Mike would have kept the other guys asleep until we pulled it out. But not tonight.

Again he didn't look right to me, again he looked like he was pushing the ball. They got two runs off him in the eighth and two more in the ninth and down we went.

The team ate the free pizza without Mike and me. We didn't eat anything at all. We dressed slowly and were the last to leave the clubhouse, walking out of the darkened ball park, heading nowhere in particular. We kind of shambled along a dirt road behind town, passing a little patch of land where tobacco was raised.

"Well, roomie," Mike finally said after about fifteen minutes of quiet, "it still hurts."

"What are you going to do?" I asked.

"I don't know."

"You ought to tell Upshot."

"Uh-uh," he said stubbornly. "That's the last thing I want to do. They'll pack me right up. He's carrying only six pitchers; he can't afford a sore arm."

"But you can't pitch."

"I'll work it out."

"You're crazy. You could do permanent damage."

"I don't think so. These things work themselves out. Lots of guys pitch with sore arms. Some guys go through a whole big league career with a bad arm."

"Where'd you hear that?"

He shrugged.

We sat on the rail fence that measured off the tobacco patch. There were crickets in the grass, beeping away with a kind of innocence that sweetened the night air.

"Listen," I said, "tell Upshot you want to miss a few turns. That can't do any harm. Maybe a week's rest is just what you need."

"Uh-uh," he said. "Once you have a history of arm trouble they don't trust you anymore."

"How bad does it hurt?"

"Not so bad."

"Liar."

"You just keep quiet about it, huh, sonny?"

"It's your arm," I said.

The club got a real reaming from Upshot before the next game. After we had suited up he locked the clubhouse door and told us to sit down. Then he really tore into us.

"You're playing lousy and you're thinking lousy," he said. "You've forgotten that you're professionals and are supposed to play like professionals. You've forgotten that you're supposed to win. You go out there every night and instead of ballplayers you look like a bunch of clowns in pajamas. You're forgetting what the purpose of this game is: to win. Some of you are hitting .200 and some of you are hitting over .300." (That last was me; I was the only one on the club over .300.)

"But you're all playing the same game," he went on, walking back and forth in front of the little space in the corner where his desk was, his hands on his hips, his eyes picking us out one by one. "You're not thinking about winning. You've accepted the fact of losing. If you're not winners then you might just as well pack up now and forget pro baseball. Because you play this game for only one thing: winning. Not glory, not headlines, not free pizza pies: but winning—which translates into money, if you're interested."

He glared at us for a few seconds. Then he said, "That's it. Now get out on the field. There's still half a season to go. You want to stick in this game, *win*."

The door was unlocked and as we started to file out, he said,

"Delaney, I want to talk to you."

I gave Mike a look and he winked at me. Then I trotted out to the field, where the lights had just been turned on, out again to another night of professional baseball. It was still the greatest game in the world, and knowing that you had to try to win every time out, why, that just took away any foolishness there might be about it.

"What'd he say?" I asked Mike when he came out.

"He asked me what was wrong."

About time, I thought.

"You tell him?" I asked.

"I told him there wasn't anything wrong, that I was just due for a few bad games, that's all. He said there isn't any such thing, that nobody is ever 'due' for anything, except a ticket home if he doesn't deliver."

"Hell, you really can't win every day," I said.

"Tell him that."

"You should've told him you were hurting."

"It feels better," Mike said.

I didn't believe him.

·13·

I'D NEVER HEARD MY FATHER SOUND SO CHEERY ON THE phone, especially with another collect call in his ear.

"How's the batting average?" he asked.

"Three sixty-two, as of this morning," I said.

"Up seven points since the last time, eh?"

He sounded like a man reporting on the stock market.

"The experts around here tell me that's pretty impressive," he said.

"They're right," I said.

"We're planning a trip down to see you soon."

"You are?" I asked.

I was glad to hear that. Actually, I'd been getting lonesome for them.

"Will you drive down?" I asked.

"We'll be coming by bus," he said.

"By bus?"

"Thirty of us."

"Thirty?" I didn't know what he was talking about.

"A lot of people from town want to see you play. There might be as many as forty of us. We're going to charter a bus."

I didn't know what to say. I wasn't happy about the idea of seeing half the town all of a sudden. For some reason or other I suddenly had the peculiar feeling that I wouldn't be able to hit a lick with all of them watching me, and that every time I popped out they would cheer, thinking it was something great. It was dumb, but that was what I thought.

"Charter a bus?" I said. I had to say something.

"We're too poor to charter a jet," he said with a laugh.

"When is this going to happen?" I asked.

"In a few weeks. We're trying to put it together, making sure everybody can get away at the same time. We want to stay a few days. Say, listen, keep hitting that average. Everybody is expecting to see another Babe Ruth. How many home runs do you have now?" He said "home runs" with an emphasis on the first word, which sounded funny.

"Seventeen," I said.

"That's good, isn't it?"

"A guy on Mt. Carleton's got twenty-six."

"Find out what he eats for breakfast," he said with a big laugh. Then he told me he'd be in touch soon again and hung up.

"I think I'll be afraid to meet your father," Susannah said.

"Why?" I asked.

She shrugged. "I don't know. Just from the way you've made him sound."

"Well," I said, "I don't know how I've made him sound, but he's really a very nice guy."

We were sitting in the afternoon sunshine, in the empty grandstand of the ballpark. For some reason or other I always liked to come to an empty ball field when I had something I wanted to think about. It was where I felt most at home, I guess, the way an actor might feel on an empty stage.

"You don't want him to come down here, do you?" Susannah asked.

"What makes you say that?" I asked. Hearing her say it annoyed me, and not because she was wrong but because she'd come closer to the truth than was comfortable.

"You just don't seem happy about it," she said. "Here, you haven't seen your family for months, and ever since you mentioned that they'd be coming down you've been glum."

"Well, maybe so," I admitted.

"Don't you want to see them?"

"I guess I do."

It wasn't that I didn't want to see them. I missed my parents and my brother. I did want to see them. It was just that I didn't want to see a whole busload of people at the same time. And it wasn't that I had anything against those people either; after all, they were friends. I just didn't like the whole *spirit* of the visit. All of a sudden my father knew my batting average, all of a sudden he was taking this big interest and showing this pride. It was like he was coming down here to show me off to everybody rather than making a visit because he wanted to see me.

It was nice that he was finally showing the interest. But it seemed to me it was based on a batting average and a lot of home runs—which was okay but which wasn't the whole story.

"I'll tell you what's bothering me," I said. "Would he be coming down if I was batting .215?"

Maybe my thinking was crazy. After all, wasn't I doing better than I thought I could simply because I had been determined to prove myself to him?

But that was wrong too. That was no way to play ball. That was no reason to hit. There were better reasons. You should be playing ball in order to impress the team and the manager and the organization, to show that the scout who had faith in you was right. You should be playing ball to help yourself, and above all, you should be doing it with all that determination because you loved it . . . not because you wanted to prove something to your father.

Susannah gave a little laugh.

"Well," she said, "if you feel that way, maybe if you stopped hitting, he wouldn't come."

I got mad, not at her, but at the idea.

"I'll never stop hitting," I said. "Not for anything. Listen, stop having such crazy ideas."

Stop hitting? The idea got me mad and kept me mad. That night, in a home game, batting against a guy named

Wilce Hatton, the best fast-ball pitcher in the league, I pounded one of my longest home runs ever.

Stop hitting? What about the free pizza pies? What about getting invited to dinner at homes all over Wyattville and seeing how pleased people were to have me? What about seeing my picture in the paper all the time and listening to the fans cheer me?

Stop hitting? What about all the people who I didn't know who said, "Way to go, Teddy" to me on the street? What about those reports to the big club that Pulski was sending out after every game? What about looking at that nice ripe, rich batting average in the paper every morning?

And what about just lying in bed at night and thinking—thinking of hitting and fielding and running and throwing? And what about the always-fresh dream that I'd had since I was five years old, of playing in the big leagues?

Stop hitting? Why, that was up to the opposing pitcher, wasn't it?

·14·

When I opened my eyes I saw mike standing in front of the bureau mirror, staring at himself. He had dressed and was holding a comb in his right hand. He was standing very still. I watched him for nearly a minute, not saying anything, because he was standing *so* still that I felt almost like an intruder on his privacy.

He'd been rocked again last night, after getting by for five innings on slow curves. He was able to hang in for that long only because the hitters were still looking for his fast ball, which he was able to throw once in a while, but then just to set them up. From where I was, standing out in center field, it seemed to me that the fast ball didn't have the zip to it that it should have had, and that whenever he threw it he kept it out of the strike zone.

I guess on a team that was going better than we were, Mike's problems would have been noticed more; but since we were losers all the time, his getting ripped the way he was seemed almost natural. Even with his bad arm, he still looked better than most of our pitchers (the rest of us had nicknamed the staff the Suicide Squad because of the line drives that were hit back at them).

Now Mike's eye caught mine in the mirror.

"Good morning, sonny," I said.

"I can't comb my hair," he said.

He had the comb in his hand and his arm raised no higher than his shoulder.

You hear about things like that. An arm so dead you can stick a fork into it, or an arm so painful you can't lift it to comb your hair.

"You know what hurts as much as the arm?" he said. I waited. "It's the way I hurt it: pushing a wooden merry-go-round. I didn't even wreck it throwing or sliding or anything like that."

He turned around and looked at me. His face, always so bright and full of mischief, was very sad. It made him seem years older.

"There's no dignity to it," he said.

"You'll work it out," I said, saying that on purpose—giving him his own line.

He shook his head.

"I don't know," he said.

"Tell Upshot. Take some time off."

"Can't do that. They'll send me home."

"You'll come back next year, good as new."

"I told you, they don't like pitchers with a history like that. It sticks with you."

"What they like even less," I said, "is pitchers who don't win."

"Nobody is winning."

"That's right," I said, folding my hands behind my

head. "And where do you think these guys are going to be next year?—They're going to be pitching on sandlots with 'Joe's Garage' stenciled on the backs of their uniforms."

"The garage in my town is owned by Harry." His face was still too sad for him to be making a joke.

"Mike Delaney, star pitcher for Harry's Garage. On the mound every Sunday. People will say, 'He used to be in the minors'."

"Shut up," he said.

"He hurt his arm, they'll say."

"Shut up."

"Never used to have that fat beer belly."

"I said, shut up."

"Tell Upshot," I said.

"No. Maybe it'll work out."

"Today you can't comb your hair. Tomorrow you won't be able to brush your teeth. Pretty soon you won't be able to lace your spikes."

"What are you, the team chaplain?"

"I'm your friend."

Now he walked over and sat on his bed, staring down at the comb in his hand. He had a look in his face of absolute helplessness and misery, as if he'd just watched his house burn down.

"You know what it feels like?" he asked. "It feels like the strongest man in the world is squeezing his fingers on it with all his strength."

"What will you do?" I asked.

He shrugged.

I wished I could help him. His whole life lay in the power of that arm, all of his hopes and dreams—which I could understand because they were my hopes and dreams too.

"It really hurts, Ted," he said.

"Maybe if you put something on it—"

"The pain feels like it's in the bone." He shook his head. "I knew this was gonna happen," he said. "I just knew it."

There were a thousand things going through his mind. He'd planned to be a ballplayer. He had no other ambition, no other preparation for his life. He wasn't interested in anything except pitching. If something happened to me, at least I could become a lawyer.

Maybe it was thinking that thing about becoming a lawyer that made me do it. I could remember time and again my father saying how he had to plead a case that, for one reason or another, made him unhappy, but that he had to do it because it was his job, his responsibility. Well, I certainly didn't want to be a lawyer, but maybe after having lived with it all my life some of it had rubbed off. You might say I had no business doing what I did, that it wasn't any of my affair. I might not have been a lawyer but surely I was a friend, and that involves some responsibility too.

I knew where Upshot had breakfast every morning. He didn't eat in Watson's, because that's where the players went, and he didn't like to get too close to them, especially with this club, when he was having to cut so many guys in mid-season.

He was sitting in a small, quiet, back-street restaurant named Sidney's, staring into his bacon and eggs. I felt sorry for him. He was a good guy stuck with a bad team, through no fault of his own. He was a good baseball man, always willing to take time to work with a player. But there's only so much you can do with a ballplayer who doesn't really have it.

He seemed glad to see me when I joined him in his booth.

"Can I talk to you about something, Skip?" I asked.

"Sure," he said.

"It's about Mike."

He drank his coffee, staring at me over the rim of the cup.

"His arm's killing him," I said.

"Since when?"

"A few weeks now."

"That stupid kid," he said shaking his head. "Why didn't he tell me? He's got so much talent. Why are they afraid to admit it when something's hurting them? Don't they know that as a professional it's expected of them? They think they're being tough, when all they're really doing is hurting themselves and the team. Do you know what he's been telling me?"

"No."

"First he told me he had hay fever, then he told me his father's been sick and that was worrying him."

"His father's healthy as a horse," I said. "And if he's got hay fever, then it's his arm that's doing the sneezing."

"The upshot of pitching with a bad arm," said Upshot, "is to ruin it forever. How'd he hurt it?"

I just stared at him, tongue-tied.

But he went right on.

"I've suspected something was wrong with him," he said. "I should have known what it was. Damn it, young ballplayers have no sense. None of you have any sense. So what if you have to sit out a few games or a few weeks, or even half a season? It's better than playing the rest of your life for . . . for . . ."

"Joe's Garage," I said.

"That's right," he said. "I'll notify the front office. He's too good a prospect to ruin."

"What'll they do?"

"Get him to a doctor, then tell him to take it easy until next spring. Chances are he'll be okay then."

"Can't you keep him, as a pinch runner or something?"

Pulski shook his head.

"He'll be sent home with orders not to look at a baseball until next spring. How'd you say he hurt himself?"

Again I just stared at him. Then I wet my lips, and said, "Sliding into third."

"You had no right to do it," Mike said. He was so mad he had tears in his eyes.

We were walking on one of the country roads behind town, just a tree-lined dirt road with no houses.

"I had to do it," I said. "You were wrecking yourself."

"It was getting better," he said. "It was feeling better each day. Now you've gone and done it. Sure they'll send me home, and I'll never hear from them again and nobody else will want to sign me."

"He said they'll send you to a doctor and that lots of rest will probably fix you up as good as new, that you were too good a prospect to ruin."

"I know why you did it," he said, really angry now. "You were jealous. You want to be the big star all by yourself. That's right, isn't it?"

"No it isn't," I said, getting angry myself now. "You know better than that. If you had kept on pitching you would've finished yourself for good. You want to have to stand on your head to comb your hair? Since you didn't have the brains or the guts to tell him, then somebody had to do it for you."

"Don't tell me I don't have guts," he yelled. I thought he was going to take a sock at me. He kicked a rock in the road with such force that it went bouncing up into the trees and a little cloud of dust swirled around his feet.

"Maybe you have guts, but you don't have any common sense."

"Maybe not, but at least I'm loyal to my friends."

"I'd have wanted you to do the same for me."

"You can afford to be a hero," he said. "You're having a good year. You don't care about anybody else."

"It seems to me you were having a good year too—until you hurt yourself. Keep on the way you're going and you'll be with Harry's Garage for sure. And you're too good for that. You've got your whole life ahead of you. Upshot said it was the professional thing to tell the manager when you're hurting. You should have told him right off. He would have sat you down for a few turns and maybe you would have been okay. But no. You were too thick-headed."

We walked quietly for a while, staring down at the road. It seemed cars didn't come this way very often.

I'd never had such an argument with a friend and I felt very bad about it. But I still felt I'd done the right thing.

After about five minutes of silence, he said, "What am I gonna tell my father?"

"The truth."

"That I was pushing a merry-go-round? He'd break my neck."

"As long as he doesn't touch your arm."

Then he stopped. We both stopped.

"Listen," he said. His tone of voice had changed; the anger was gone, and there was a certain wariness in it. "What'd you tell Upshot happened?"

"That you hurt it sliding into third."

He rubbed his chin for a moment, gazing off into space. Then he looked at me.

"That's it then," he said. "That's going to be the story. I clubbed a double, a bullet of a line drive into right center. I decided to stretch it into three. I went cutting around second, heading for third. The coach fell on the ground, which was the signal to slide. The relay came in at the same time I did. I hit the dirt head first, coming in real hard, and jammed my shoulder into the bag."

"You safe or out?"

He thought about it for a moment.

"Out," he said. "I don't have any triples this year."

The story made him feel better. I could see him sitting around his home town all winter telling everybody about his terrific slide into third base, and how he had pitched on sheer guts after that, until he had gone to the skipper and said he couldn't go on any longer, that he was hurting the team.

"Listen," he said as we walked back to our rooming house, "I'm sorry for what I said. I got excited; I didn't mean those things."

"Forget it," I said.

"You did the right thing. I would've done the same."

I gave him a sly grin, and said, "I was only getting even with you for getting me arrested in spring training."

He shook his head.

"Boy, Teddy," he said, "we've done some stupid things."

He took a bus out that afternoon. I sat with him on the wooden bench in front of the drug store, where the bus stopped. It would take him through Kentucky and then home to Ohio. His two pieces of luggage stood in front of us on the sidewalk.

"So," he said, "who's gonna look after you now?"

"I'll have to manage," I said.

"You know something? Ever since I knew I was going home, my arm hasn't hurt a bit. Maybe the trouble was in my head all the time. That's possible, you know. I read it once."

"Then instead of not using your arm until next spring, don't use your head. That should be easy for you."

"Ah, sonny," he said, "you never appreciated me. You'll miss me."

"Say, you'll write, won't you?" I asked.

"Sure. You?"

"Sure. I'll send you some clips, let you know how we're doing."

He glanced at his watch.

"Well, soon," he said looking along Main Street, to where the bus would appear on the mountain road, big and sleek and cool, and scoop him up and carry him out of Wyattville. I couldn't help wondering if I'd ever see him again. Baseball is like that; you make friends, and then they're gone. I was hoping the bus would be late.

"We'll get together in spring training," I said.

"Sure," he said. "I'll be there."

"You'll be a better pitcher because of what you've learned this year."

"Yeah," he said sourly: "don't push merry-go-rounds."

"It won't be the same without you here."

"You know, I just thought of something: what am I gonna do for the rest of the summer if I can't play ball?" He had a very confused look in his face. "I mean, I've been playing baseball every summer ever since I could walk. Here it's still only June. What do I do?"

He shook his head and looked down at his shoes. He had polished them for the trip home. He was wearing a jacket and tie. It was the first time I'd seen the tie; I hadn't even known he owned one. I guess he wanted to go home looking like a professional.

Two kids walked by slowly, looking at us. They stopped near the bench, staring.

"Hi, Ted," one said.

We turned around. I didn't know them.

"Hi," I said.

They grinned.

"Hello, men," Mike said.

They didn't seem to know who he was.

"You know me," he said. "I used to be Mike Delaney."

"Hi, Mike," one said, then they walked away.

We saw the bus coming down from the mountains then, very small at first, like it could fit into your fist. But it was getting bigger. Mike wet his lips, then took a deep breath and sighed. He stood up and held out his hand.

"Okay, sonny," he said.

We shook hands, and then he picked up his luggage. The bus came alongside and rolled to a halt, the door already open. Mike climbed aboard and I sort of walked along with him as he headed through the bus looking for a seat. The driver paused until Mike got settled and I saw the old pitcher wrestling to get his luggage up on the rack. It took him longer than it should have. I guess the arm was hurting. Then he took a window seat, looking down at me. The bus started up and as it rolled away I grinned and waved. He just pressed his lips together and nodded his head. You could tell how badly he didn't want to go.

I watched until the bus had gone, until its big broad backside was no bigger than a postage stamp on the highway.

· 15 ·

AFTER MIKE HAD GONE, AND I REALLY MISSED HIM, I GUESS I
had more time to think about myself. I didn't want another roommate, because I had once read somewhere
that the big league superstars had the special privilege of
rooming alone if they chose. So, because I was feeling
pretty sure-headed these days and because I thought I
was a superstar, even if only in the South Virginia
League, I didn't get another roommate.

My birthday came at the end of June and Susannah
showed up at the house one afternoon with a present. It
was wrapped in blue paper and from the shape of it I
knew it was either a box of candy or a book. She sat next
to me on the porch steps while I undid the wrappings.

It was a book. It was called *The Science of Good Hitting,* and was put together by a half dozen of the best hitters in the big leagues.

"What's this for?" I asked.

"It's for your birthday," she said.

"No, I mean, why'd you buy this particular book?"

"Because it's on baseball."

"Look," I said, "I know it's on baseball. But of all
things, why a book on hitting?"

"Because the man in the store said it was by experts."

"Did you tell him it was for me?"

"No."

"Well, I'm glad of that," I said.

"Why? What's the difference?"

"Because I'd look foolish. Look, I'm hitting .352; I don't need a book on hitting."

She was hurt.

"But it's by experts," she said.

"What's the matter, don't you think I know my game?"

"I thought you'd like it," she said unhappily.

Now I saw how bad she felt. I kissed her on the cheek.

"I do like it," I said. "I really do. It's just that . . . no, I really do like it."

A book on hitting. I thought that was pretty funny. That's like giving a bird a book on flying, or a fish a book on swimming. Either you do it or you don't. They can tell you to keep your eye on the ball and hold your elbows away from your body and to feel comfortable up at the plate. But they can't step in there and swing for you. That you've got to do by yourself. And that I was doing.

I went on a tear right after Mike left. Through our next seven games I went thirteen for twenty-eight, including two more home runs. We lost five of those games, but I didn't care anymore. I was concentrating on myself. Once I even swung through a "take" sign, which made Upshot sore, even though I got a base hit.

I doubt whether a guy can be happier than I was those weeks. After every game there'd be a few people waiting for autographs, and not just kids either, but older people too. I was getting invited to dinner three or four nights a week. I couldn't walk down the street without getting a hello every thirty seconds. And the local fans cheered just about everything I did on the ball field.

One night I caught a couple of flies in center field with one hand. I'd watched some big league outfielders on television do it and didn't see anything wrong with it. But later, in the clubhouse, a few of the guys called me "Showboat." They were kidding, but all the same I didn't like it. I didn't think there was anything wrong in grabbing a ball as easy as you could, as long as you didn't drop it.

I started to feel separate from the rest of the team. There wasn't a guy on it who was doing anything. Our next highest hitter after me was Charley Garelli the first baseman, with .282. I was the only one in double figures in homers. Then, when attendance started to fall off, the paper ran a story in which it said, "And if it wasn't for Ted Marshall, probably nobody would come to a game. It's the worst Wyattville team in years—except for Teddy."

I couldn't tell if any of the guys resented it or not. I guess some did, human nature being what it is. But I didn't care. It was every man for himself.

And then one morning Upshot called me at the house. It was the first time he'd done that all season.

"Come over to the office," he said.

As I walked into town I was wondering what it could be about. I thought maybe I'd missed a sign again last night. I knew that a few times up at the plate I'd barely looked down at the third base coach to see if anything was on. Upshot never had me bunting, so I didn't have to worry about that, but sometimes he put the hit-and-run on. Herb Markson had been thrown out stealing during one of my times at bat, and maybe I'd missed the hit-and-run then. If that was it, it was going to cost me five dollars.

Pulski was sitting alone in the office when I walked in, his feet up on the desk. He didn't tell me to sit down or anything. He just looked at me for a couple of seconds. Then he said,

"Pack your bags, Ted. You're going up."

It was funny. I'd been thinking about that every day for the last month. Some of the guys had been joking about it, about me going to Seltonia; but for some reason or other it hadn't been in my mind that morning. So it hit me with full impact, a real surprise. I think I smiled a little, but otherwise tried not to show anything.

"When do I leave?" I asked.

"There's a bus out of here at four. Can you be ready by then?" Now he had a soft, wise smile in the corners of his mouth.

The clock on the wall said eleven-thirty.

"I'll make it," I said.

"I figured you could. Now go ahead and pack."

The first thing I did was call my father at his office. I told him to forget about Wyattville and come instead to Seltonia. He seemed kind of confused until I told him it was a big, important promotion, and that they only moved up the best players in mid-season.

"Where is Seltonia?" he asked.

"Pennsylvania."

"That's a big state."

"Look on the map."

"We'll find it."

"It's not as far as Wyattville."

"Makes no difference," he said. "Everybody's coming to see America's best ballplayer; distance means nothing."

He told me the big trip would take place in a few weeks, that they had chartered the bus, and that so far about forty people had signed up. I still didn't like the idea of it, but I didn't say anything.

Then I called Susannah. I was so happy and excited about moving up to B ball that I didn't realize she might not like the idea.

"I'm going to miss you," she said.

It was a peculiar feeling, one that I wouldn't have thought possible. If anybody had said to me that I'd be leaving Wyattville and not think of missing Susannah, I would have thought them crazy. I really liked her a lot, but all of a sudden that didn't seem to matter. The only thing that mattered was going to Seltonia. I think she sensed it in my voice.

"Will you miss me?" she asked over the telephone.

"Sure," I said. "Of course."

But even as I was talking to her the only thing really on my mind was packing my bags and getting on that bus.

"Meet me at the bus," I told her and hung up.

A lot of people came to see me off, including about half the team. There must've been a crowd of fifty people waiting with me. Everybody kept shaking my hand and wishing me luck and telling me to remember them when I was a big league star. I looked up once and saw Upshot watching me from the window of the team office. I waved to him and he nodded.

Then the bus came rolling down out of the mountains and into town. The last time I'd thought about the bus, it had been a sad occasion. That was when Mike had left, and there had been just the two of us waiting that time. Man, it's different when you go off a hero.

There were big cheers and a lot of yelling when I got on the bus, and the other passengers must have wondered who I was. I sat by the window waving to everybody until the bus pulled away.

Then I sat back in my seat, my hands folded on my belt buckle, a silly half-smile on my face. All of a sudden I couldn't believe what was happening, because for some reason what came flooding through my mind were all the doubts I had had in spring training about making the team. Then I realized how foolish all of that had been, how foolish it was to doubt yourself when you knew you had the talent.

It wasn't until about fifteen minutes later that it occurred to me that Susannah hadn't come down to the bus stop to say goodbye.

·16·

I'LL TELL YOU WHAT THE FIRST THING I NOTICED WAS WHEN I walked into the Seltonia clubhouse. It wasn't that they had lockers, or that the showers were in a separate part of the clubhouse. It was that the guys seemed so much older. Maybe at that age people do—I wasn't eighteen yet and most of these guys seemed at least two or three years older. Or maybe it wasn't so much the age difference as that they were more experienced ballplayers. For most of them it was their second year in pro ball, and for some it was their third.

I'd ridden the bus most of the night, hardly getting any sleep, though that didn't bother me. I hadn't wanted to sleep; my thoughts were too happily excited to blank out with sleep. The way I was figuring it, if I could keep hitting the rest of this season, I might get a shot at an even higher classification next year, one from which they sometimes promote you right into the bigs. Why, this time next year I could be on my way to the big leagues. Try and sleep with *that* idea in your head.

When I got into town I went straight to the team office. I sat around there for awhile talking to the business manager. He told me they were looking forward to my getting there, that they had known I was going to be sent up. Seltonia was in third place in the league, with an outside chance of finishing on top, but what they needed was another stick in the lineup.

"Well," I said, "that's me." I was feeling pretty good.

"The pitching here is tougher than what you've been seeing," I was told.

"We'll see what happens."

"Yes, that's about all we can do," he said.

He drove me out to the ball park, where they were playing that night. I met Frank DeLucca, the manager. He was a playing manager. He was kind of short, with dark features, a handshake like iron, and a clipped way of talking, like he didn't want to waste breath.

"You just come in?" he asked.

"Yes," I said.

"Want to take it easy tonight?"

"No, I feel great."

"All right. We'll get you a suit."

DeLucca started introducing me to the players, then lost interest in it and one of the guys finished the job. I said hello to and shook the hands of the whole team. I recognized some of the names, from following the team in *The Sporting News*. Some of the players, the stars, I had fixed in my mind as looking a certain way. I was wrong each time. In fact one guy, Borden, who had already stolen forty-five bases and whom I had imagined to be tall and lean as a rail, turned out to be a black guy who was built stocky.

"How's Wyattville?" somebody asked me.

"It's still there," I said.

"Watson still giving out the pizzas?" another one asked.

"Sure. You play there last year?"

"Yeah."

"How many you hit?" I asked.

"Six," he said.

Now I felt funny. I'd hit twenty home runs when I left, but I didn't want to just yell it out. You don't like to do that, especially when you're a stranger, and even more especially when the people around you are older and more experienced.

I had a peculiar feeling as I suited up. It was like I was starting all over again; overnight, I had gone from being the star of the team to being just another guy who was going to have to start from scratch and prove himself. What I had done in Wyattville meant nothing to these guys. Some of them had played there and been promoted to Seltonia, so that was all behind them. They had already done what I had; it was up to me to do what they were doing.

My new teammates were nice enough. Most of them went out of their way to make me feel welcome. They talked to me about the league, the pitching, the lights in the different parks.

It wasn't until I took batting practice that I realized how tired I was. As anxious as I felt to play, I was almost sorry I'd told DeLucca I was ready. But when I stepped into the cage to take my five swings I noticed a pepper game down the line come to a halt, and that some guys who were throwing stopped. With my new teammates looking on with such interest and curiosity, it became more than just batting practice.

The pitcher, a right-hander, was throwing with good speed, but mainly for control. I hit his second pitch off the right field wall. I hit each ball sharply, and when I was finished the pepper game started again and so did the throwing. I felt pretty good.

I felt even better after my first time up for Seltonia. They had me batting seventh (I'd never hit that far down in my life), against a side-wheeling left-hander. He was tough on lefties, and I guess DeLucca wanted to know right off what I could do against a pitcher like that. The guy was fast, with a good slider that he threw right in on the hands. He knew I was new here, and with his first pitch he brushed me back. It was a fast ball and really dusted the letters on my shirt. Then he had me bailing out with a big curve that broke over for a strike. He came back with the slider and I hit it over the first base-man's head and down the line for two.

Standing on second, I felt real good. Some loud-voiced guy in the stands yelled out,

"Hey, New Guy! You're all right!"

The rest of the game wasn't so much fun. The lefty

went all the way, and each time I came up he worked a pattern on me. He kept the fast ball just out of the strike zone, set me up with sliders, then struck me out with an overhand curve that broke straight down from the shoulders to the knees. He struck me out three times. I'd never seen a curve like that.

Seltonia had a little more life than Wyattville, even though the surrounding area wasn't as pretty. We were more or less in the middle of a coal mining area and some of the countryside was depressing. About a mile or two outside of town there was a steel mill and when the wind was blowing in the wrong direction the air could get very dirty. I'd heard about air pollution, but I'd never really lived in it. Now I was able to get some idea of what people were talking about. Waking up in the morning I'd sometimes find little pieces of soot on the sheets and on my clothes.

"The air gets so heavy sometimes," Rick Afton, my roommate, said, "that the ball doesn't travel so good."

"You mean I've got to worry about that too?" I asked.

"Sure," he said. Then he shrugged. "It gives you an excuse, if you want one."

Well, I don't know if I wanted an excuse or not. The air wasn't getting in the way of my long shots, and that was because I wasn't getting any long shots. After six games I had only four hits to show for twenty-seven at bats. But DeLucca kept playing me. I guess he had orders from upstairs. When I joined the team they made an outfielder named Carlos Vesquez sit down to give me a chance. He was hitting .265, but they wanted to see what I could do.

DeLucca told me after one game to show up for batting practice the next morning.

"We'll get you untracked," he said. "Don't worry."

One of our right-handers, a big blonde guy named Fletcher, was going to throw to me, with a bunch of local kids scattered around to field the balls. Fletcher was on a five-day league suspension for shoving an umpire, so he was free to pitch.

I'll show you how a guy can get a wrong impression. I thought that maybe Fletcher didn't like me for some reason or other. Sometimes that happens: you just look at a guy and take a dislike to him. Anyway, that was what I thought. Because that big guy stood out there and fired bullets for fifteen minutes, and I could barely get around on most of them. I knew what was coming, too, because DeLucca was standing behind the cage yelling fast ball. And that was what Fletcher threw, fast balls, the likes of which I had never seen. And even with setting myself for them, I still couldn't do much.

Then DeLucca went out to throw. He mixed fast balls with curves and while he wasn't a pitcher, he had pretty good stuff. I tagged him hard, hitting a few over the fence, and that made me feel better.

Later, I sat in the clubhouse with DeLucca.

"Hey," I said, trying to make a joke, "is Fletcher sore at me or something?"

"No," the manager said. "Why?"

"He was really pumping."

"That's the way he throws."

"Maybe I ought to choke up a little against a guy like that."

He shook his head.

"You swing the way you've been swinging," he said.

"I couldn't hit him," I said.

"I noticed," he said.

I was having a sandwich with Rick Afton before that night's game.

"Listen," I said, "what's Fletcher's record this year?"

"Fletcher?" he asked. "Oh, he's about seven and seven."

"You mean he's lost seven games?" I couldn't believe it.

"He gets hit hard sometimes," Afton said.

By whom? I wondered.

I had my first good game that night. I got three singles, and even thought two of them were bleeders that I legged out, I was willing to take them. The next day, a Sunday doubleheader, I poled my first home run for Seltonia, a long fly over the right field fence. It was the only hit I got all day, but I felt pretty good about it.

I called home that night and told my father about the home run.

"That's great," he said. "Listen, save some for when we get there. We'll be there in about two weeks."

"This town isn't so attractive," I said. "It's coal mining country." I said that without thinking, but I knew why I said it: I still wasn't happy about him bringing all those people to see me.

"We don't care about that," he said.

"It's pretty ugly. No place for a vacation."

"We're coming to see a great ballplayer," he said.

Great ballplayer? I thought. I was glad he didn't ask my batting average. It was so low it had roots. Like .211.

· 17 ·

A LETTER FROM SUSANNAH MADE ME HOMESICK FOR A LOT
of things, including Susannah. I don't know why I
should have missed Wyattville, but suddenly I did. It
didn't make sense, since all I'd been playing for was the
chance to move up, and here I was, moved up, and unhappy. I guess I knew what it was: I missed being the
star of the team, I missed walking down the street and
having everybody say hello to me. I missed what had
happened in Wyattville rather than Wyattville itself.
You can't pack success in your bag and take it to the next
town with you.

DeLucca had to keep playing me. That was the rough
thing. I thought that if maybe I had a chance to sit down
for a few games I might be able to get my bearings. But
he had his orders from the front office. A young ballplayer doesn't have all that much time to prove himself;
so they have to find out about you pretty fast. A good
batting average at Wyattville is important only so far as
it gets you to Seltonia; then it's a new deck.

Things got worse. They dropped me to eighth in the
lineup and sat me down altogether against certain left-

handers. Over one five-game stretch I got one hit in twenty times up. My average dipped under .200.

The other guys felt sorry for me. There wasn't much they could do, but I had their sympathy. DeLucca was losing patience though. We were losing too many games, and a good part of it was my fault.

The pitching was too good, that's all there was to it. It wasn't just that the pitchers were faster and had better breaking stuff—I'd unloaded on some pretty good pitchers in Wyattville—it was that they had better control. They hit their spots more often, they were smarter. These were guys with two or more years in pro ball. When you play ball at those levels, one year's experience can make a world of difference. I knew for myself how much I'd learned in spring training and throughout the first half of the year. And here were guys with twice that much experience.

I was getting to know how some of those weak sisters in the Wyattville lineup felt. Boy, it's not much of a feeling, I can tell you; all emptiness and rainy days inside you. The world seems cold and you resent it any time you see somebody laughing.

I met DeLucca on the street one afternoon. He wasn't the friendliest guy in the world to begin with, and with me going the way I was, he seemed even worse.

"Front office wants to know what's wrong with you," he said. We were standing in front of a hardware store.

"I'm not hitting," I said. That was like a fish saying it was wet.

"I've noticed," he said. "You feeling okay?"

"No complaints," I said. I could've said I had a stiff shoulder or something, but I didn't. You can live on excuses for only so long.

"They want me to keep playing you," he said.

"Okay with me," I said.

"This league too fast for you?"

I didn't know what to say to that. Obviously something here was too fast for me. He was putting me on the spot with a dumb question.

"I'm trying my best," I said.

"I know you are," he said in that quick little way he had of talking. "Well, maybe you'll come around."

"I've never been in such a slump in my life." But he knew, and I knew, that there was a difference between being in a slump and being in a league that was too fast for you.

"Shouldn't have slumps like that in the minors," he said. "I'm giving you some inside information: they expect you to keep hitting."

"I'll hit," I said.

"Good," he said. "Okay."

I watched him walk away, while I leaned on a parking meter in front of the hardware store. I stayed there about a half hour, thinking about nothing in particular. Nobody said hello to me the whole time.

I just stopped hitting. The inside of my head turned to pure confusion from it. I even sneaked off to a doctor one day to have a check-up, figuring that maybe the problem was physical. The doctor checked my eyes, my blood pressure, my heart, my reflexes.

"You seem to be in perfect health," he said when he was through with the examination.

"I do?" I think I must have looked disappointed.

"Are you feeling all right?"

"I suppose so."

"Anything hurt?" he asked.

"No."

"Appetite all right?"

"Fine."

"Getting enough sleep?"

"Plenty."

"Then what seems to be your problem?" he asked.

What could I say to him—that I wasn't hitting? What could he possibly prescribe—a lighter bat, a different batting stance? So I told him I had just wanted a checkup, and he told me it was always a good idea to do that. As I walked out of his office I had the feeling he was giving me a strange look.

I may have been eating and sleeping enough, but I wasn't enjoying it. I wasn't enjoying anything, not a movie or television or reading. My mind remained stuck on the problem. There was no getting away from it, because every night I had to go out and play another ball game and face it again.

You get to feel dumb after awhile. You're being paid to do something, you want to do it, you know you can— but you're not doing it. All of a sudden something that you've been doing so well all your life, been doing without even thinking about it, stops becoming so easy. And worse than that, it had stopped being fun. I never thought I'd ever see the day when I'd dread going out to play ball. It was like some old friend had betrayed me.

It got worse. I started to press at the plate. I no longer felt natural. I went up on the handle a little; I went for the lighter bat; I moved around in the box; I crouched; I straightened up. Nothing helped. Those fast balls kept exploding on me, those curves kept snapping on the corners or across the knees—anyplace and everyplace, except where I was swinging.

This wasn't like any other failure I'd ever experienced. Sometimes I had failed in school, or at some project I was trying, or one thing or another. But none of it ever bothered me. But now I was failing at the one thing I loved to do. That's more than failure—that's *misery*.

It was a very tough thing for me to do to adjust to the fact that I wasn't hitting. You look at your batting average and you don't believe what you see, because in your arms and legs you are feeling much better than that average. You go out to the ball park and go through all the pregame practice and you feel fine and there's no reason in the world why you shouldn't hit, particularly since you've been hitting all your life.

That's what I told myself one night, just before a game started: There's no reason in the world why I shouldn't hit. All of a sudden I got this great big burst of confidence inside me, like the sun had come up or something, and I felt as if I had found the answer. I couldn't wait to get up to the plate.

I don't think I ever felt stronger or more confident as I did that first time at bat. The pitcher was a righty, and he threw hard. He showed me a fast ball off the corner that I let go. Then he threw me a curve. I followed the break perfectly, my eye on it all the way, strode in on it and whipped the bat.

I heard the ball slam into the catcher's glove.

I stepped out of the box for a moment. Where had that ball gone when I started my swing? I had it lined up exactly right. It was as if it turned into air the moment I swung.

I saw another curve like that and took it for a strike. Then I lay back for the fast ball, figuring he'd be trying to bite a corner with it. Well, it looked like a fast ball, except that it was a slider and at the last second it trimmed the outside corner and I was out.

It was a whole night of that. Later he tied me up with changes of speed and had me overswinging. Then came that good curve which seemed to disappear somewhere under the bat, and that hard slider which had an eye for the outside corner. I struck out three times in four at bats and popped to second the other time.

I was so sore at myself after that game I nearly cried. I knew how they were pitching me, but there wasn't anything I could do about it. What made it all so frustrating was I knew I was strong enough to send the ball out if I could hit it; but what good was the power if I couldn't make contact?

"Your head is still in Wyattville," Rick Afton said to me that night. "You're still looking for the pitches you saw in that league. Well, man, you're not going to see them, unless somebody makes a mistake."

"So what do I do?" I asked.

"Keep swinging," he said.

The people who hung around the ballplayers (you get that kind in every town) looked at me kind of funny. Or maybe it was my imagination, because I kept having the feeling I didn't belong. Had that been happening to some of those weak hitters in Wyattville? I hadn't noticed; but of course I wouldn't have, since everybody was paying attention to me, and because I was getting all the attention I didn't think to notice who wasn't getting any, and how they might have felt. But I knew now.

The worst thing was, I think, those phone conversations with my father. As the day of the visit drew closer he was getting more and more excited. We would talk and he'd ask how I was doing and I'd tell him fine. He didn't ask too many questions, so telling him the lies was easy. I kept hoping that I'd start to hit before he showed up with all those people from home.

Two days before the big visit I was benched. I knew it had to happen sooner or later and I didn't know whether to welcome it or not. If I wasn't in the lineup I couldn't strike out—that was one sure thing, and I figured it was better to be sitting down rather than playing and looking bad in front of my family and friends. I think I welcomed the benching more than I disliked it, which goes to show how far my spirits had sunk.

"What are you going to tell your old man?" Rick Afton, my roommate, asked.

"Injury," I said. I had it all worked out in my mind. I'd say I hurt my leg in my last game at Wyattville and didn't want to tell them about it when I got here for fear they'd send me back. The injury, I would say, prevented me from taking my normal stride and had thrown off my timing and everything else, and so I wasn't hitting. And finally the pain had become so bad I had to sit down.

"It's not a bad story," Rick said after I'd told him.

"What else can I do?"

"You'll get a lot of sympathy."

"With a .190 average I'll need it. Will you back me up on it?"

He shrugged. "Sure," he said.

"Maybe I'll even tape the leg, to make it look good."

He laughed.

We were in our room, playing a game of gin.

"You ever go into a slump like mine?" I asked.

He was a second baseman, with a steady bat, hitting in the .270's.

"No," he said. "Not like yours, never that bad."

"The way DeLucca talks you'd think it was against the law to have a low batting average."

"It almost is, the way they play this game."

"They forget what I did at Wyattville."

"That's right. It doesn't mean a thing. And most of the time it isn't even what you did last week, but what you did yesterday and what they think you can do tomorrow. You can't stop for a second; there are too many guys behind you. You stop hitting, even for a little while, you're in trouble. And it's not only in baseball," he said. "That's the way it is wherever you go. If a salesman stops selling or if a guy has a few bad days in the office, they're in trouble."

"But you can't keep moving ahead all the time," I said.

"You have to. That's what people want. Nobody likes a loser."

"Everybody can't be a winner."

"That's right—and that's why there are millions of people nobody ever heard of."

"Man, it's crazy," I said shaking my head.

I guess some people won't look on failure or bad times as simply hard luck or a temporary thing but instead think it's a disease that's catching. And they probably look on success the same way. Why else did everybody in Wyattville say hello to me and invite me over for dinner? It wasn't me they were taking to their hearts—it was a batting average.

"You know what?" I said to Rick. "A guy hits .350 and .190 in the same season, he becomes a philosopher."

"That's all right too," he said. "As long as he's good at it."

·18·

I HAD JUST COME OUT OF THE FIVE AND DIME WHEN ONE OF the guys told me DeLucca wanted to see me, in the team office.

I'd gone to the five and dime and bought a roll of white adhesive tape and was about to head back to my room and tape up my leg. I had decided to go ahead with the idea. Tape up your leg to save your face—something like that. The whole idea made me feel dumb, but a .190 batting average can affect the mind.

As I went up the steps to the office I decided I'd ask DeLucca to help me out by telling my father I had the bad leg and what a shame it was, since it was interfering with the development of a brilliant prospect. Once you give a lie its head it develops an imagination of its own and begins to run wild in wide-screen technicolor.

There was DeLucca sitting behind the desk, looking at me as if I'd come to deliver lunch. The man had a way of making you feel like an outcast. I wondered if Upshot would've been the same way. He hadn't seemed to be that sort, but of course he had a whole team of failures and there was no way he could ignore *everybody*.

"Hello, Skip," I said.

"Been looking for you," he said.

"Here I am."

"Sit down."

He was slouched way down in his chair. He was a strong little guy. He always wore polo shirts and they showed off his powerful arms.

"I guess you know what's up," he said.

"No, I don't," I said.

He looked at me kind of funny, like he was trying to figure me out. Maybe he thought I should have known, or maybe he thought I did know and was making believe I didn't.

"We're sending you down," he said.

"Down?"

"Back to Wyattville."

"But why?" I asked, which was the dumb question of all time. It was just that I wanted so badly not to go back to Wyattville that I actually felt for a moment that there was no good reason for me to go.

"You're not ready for this brand of ball," he said.

"That's not true," I said. "I'm just in a slump, that's all. I'll come out of it."

He shook his head.

"You've got to learn to hit the curve," he said. "They're curving you to death here."

"But what good is going back to Wyattville going to do?"

"You'll be able to keep playing. Here, I can't play you

anymore. It's not good for you. It can destroy your confidence."

"Not me," I said. "I've got plenty of confidence."

But this was just talk now, useless talk. The decision had been made; and I wasn't even talking to the man who had made that decision. These things were decided in the front office.

I don't think I ever felt so empty inside, so hopeless and defeated. DeLucca didn't say anything for a few moments. I guess he had some sympathy for me. After all, he was a ballplayer who hadn't made it all the way; there had been a day in his life when somebody had told him he was going back, that he hadn't cut it. It happens even to the best. The day has to come when they can't cut it anymore, no matter how great they've been. Even Babe Ruth had been told that he couldn't hit anymore. I felt as though I had been told that I was washed up instead of just being sent out for more seasoning.

I just sat there staring at the floor, feeling as though I'd been left out in the rain all night. Then I looked up at him and I must have had real panic in my eyes, because he frowned.

"But I can't go," I said.

"No?" he asked.

"My father, my mother, my whole damned home town are all coming here tomorrow morning."

"Can't you stop them?"

"They're on the way," I said.

"There's nothing I can do," he said.

"When do I have to leave?"

"I was going to say tonight, but you can wait till tomorrow. No later than tomorrow night. Pulski'll want you in that lineup as soon as possible."

"What's the difference?" I said. "They're not going any-place down there."

"That's the wrong attitude," he said kind of sharply. "You play ball with that kind of attitude you'll never get anywhere, I don't care if you hit .500. Sometimes you kids don't understand that. Don't you ever wonder why some guys who hit .270 make the bigs, while others who hit .350 don't? It's attitude. Give me a .270 man who'll break his neck to win ball games, and never mind the guy who says what's the difference. You'd better learn that."

He was right, no doubt of it. I was sorry for what I said.

"You listen to me," he said, sitting up now and leaning forward, resting his arms on the desk. "You've got power, speed, a great natural swing. All you need is experience and the right attitude and you'll be back. If we didn't think you had the equipment we'd be sending you home instead of back to Wyattville. So stop feeling sorry for yourself and play ball. Now clear out. I'll see you in spring training."

I walked back to my room. Okay. Everything he said was right. I'd said some dumb things because I was depressed, and he'd set me straight. You can learn to hit the curve. They can teach you that. He'd given me a good, hard-nosed lecture, something that baseball people could understand. But the problem was —my father wasn't a baseball person. How could I tell *him* I'd learn to hit the curve and that this wasn't really failure but simply lack of experience? What was I going to tell him when instead of standing in center field with the crowd cheering. I was going to be hanging around with a packed suitcase waiting for a bus?

· 19 ·

WHEN THAT CHARTERED BUS CAME ROARING INTO TOWN
the next morning I felt like a tour guide who was waiting to tell the tour that the hotel had burned down. I felt
like a fool, a failure, a traitor, and a big mountain of
hopelessness.

In fact, I wished the hotel had burned down, so they
would have to turn around and go away. I wished a lot of
desperate things. I had even been tempted to sneak out
of town the night before and leave somebody behind to
tell the tale. I was going to ask DeLucca to explain things
to my father, but then I decided against it. I had to face
it all by my lonesome.

I met them at the hotel. They all cheered when they
saw me, a whole noisy busload of people. I stood at the
door as they got off, shaking hands with each one. Some
of the men called me "Home Run Teddy." All friends
and neighbors. The grocer, the plumber, the dentist, a
couple of school teachers. What was I going to do?—Get
them all together in the main dining room and tell them
I couldn't hit the curve ball in this league?

I could've taped up my leg and limped around and

blamed it all on that. But I didn't. I didn't want to have people asking me all winter how my leg was. I was going to tell the truth. After all, I knew in my heart that I'd be back in Seltonia next year, ripping that curve ball and everything else. Sometimes you have to satisfy and fulfill yourself with what *you* know about yourself and never mind what anybody else thinks.

I went upstairs with my parents and brother and sat in their room while they unpacked.

"Well, we're here," my father said. I'd never seen him so cheerful. He was like the general of the whole crew. He'd seen to the rooms and whenever some question came up it was to him the person went.

"Have a nice trip?" I asked.

"Wonderful," he said. "We spent one night in New York, saw some of the sights in Philly, and here we are. One of the men said that the Statue of Liberty was all right, and Independence Hall was interesting, but nothing would compare to the sight of Teddy hitting one out."

My mother thought I'd lost a little weight. I had lost a few pounds, but that was nothing compared to what I'd lost off my batting average. My brother wanted to know if they'd get into the game free and whether I could get a couple of baseballs for him. He was wearing a baseball cap and seemed never to take his mitt off his hand.

I told my father I'd have to skip lunch with them because there was a team meeting. That was the only lie I told. I just didn't want to have to sit with forty people and listen to everything. I ate lunch by myself in a local restaurant, in a place where the ballplayers never went. Boy, did I have thoughts, and not just about my father and everybody else either, but about going back to Wyattville, where I'd been such a hero. What was I going to tell them there?

After showing the family where I lived (my mother thought the mattress was too soft), I told my father I wanted to talk to him.

We left the house together and walked along the street. What I had to tell him was fairly simple, but I was so unhappy about it that I didn't know how to make the words come.

Usually, when you tell somebody that you want to talk to them and then go ten minutes without saying anything, they'll ask you what's up. But my father didn't say a word. He just walked along next to me as we went in and out of the streets, waiting for me to talk. I couldn't tell if he guessed something was wrong or not.

I don't know if I did it on purpose, but I found we had walked in the direction of the ball park. I guess that was still the place where I felt most comfortable and at home, hitting or not.

We found the place completely empty when we walked in. Nothing seems as empty as an empty ball park. I guess it's because it's not intended to be that way; and a place that has known a lot of noise and cheering can't help but to look lonely in its emptiness.

We walked across the infield and stood on the

mound. My father had never been on a baseball diamond before. He asked me about the pitching rubber. I told him how the pitcher had to keep his foot on it in order to throw a legal pitch.

"Why is the mound raised?" he asked.

"To give the pitcher a little advantage."

"Why should they do that?"

I laughed. "They shouldn't. If you ask me, they should make them pitch out of a hole."

"It must be tough to hit against a man throwing from this little hill."

"Oh, it is. It's very tough."

"How fast do they throw?"

"In the big leagues they can throw it more than ninety miles an hour. Some of them can throw a curve almost that fast too."

He whistled.

"How the devil do you hit it?" he asked shaking his head.

"Well . . . you don't always hit it."

"And you don't have much time either, do you?"

"Not much more than it takes to blink an eye. You have to decide whether it's a ball or a strike, how high or low, whether it's going to stay in or out, how much it's going to move."

"Do you learn all that, or is it just a reflex?"

"Well, a lot of it is reflexes. And they can teach you. Experience helps a lot. That's what I need right now, more experience."

We walked away from the mound, heading out across the infield toward the outfield.

"Tell you the truth," I said, walking with my head down, "I haven't been doing so well here."

"You haven't?" He was surprised.

"It's been very rough."

"I guess you can't have a good day every day."

"I've had very few good days here."

"I thought you were doing so well," he said.

"Well, I haven't. As a matter of fact, they're sending me back to Wyattville."

"Back to Wyattville?" Now he stopped. We were standing in short center field. He had the most puzzled look on his face.

"I'm leaving tonight," I said.

"Tonight? But aren't we going to see you play?"

I shook my head.

"Ted," he said, "I don't understand. We thought you were doing so well."

Well, there it was. No lie can stay up in the air forever. It's got to come home to roost sometime.

"Do you realize that over forty people have come all this way to see you play?"

"I didn't hear until yesterday that I was being sent down."

"But what about all of our friends? After all, *I* was the one who . . ."

I guess I blew my stack. I couldn't help it.

"It seems to me," I said all of a sudden, before I knew

it, my voice pretty hot, "that you're worried and concerned about everybody except me. How about some thought for me? Do you think I've been enjoying myself here, looking like an utter bum at the plate? Do you think I *want* to go back to Wyattville?"

He was surprised by my tone of voice. He gave me a long and curious look.

"Why did you keep saying everything was going well?" he asked after a pause, his voice very quiet.

"Well, I thought I'd get going. But I was just never able to hit my stride."

"Do you feel all right?"

"There's nothing wrong physically. I just can't hit the pitching here."

"But you hit it in Wyattville. Is it so different?"

"Oh, it's plenty different. These guys have more experience."

"But isn't a pitch a pitch? I mean—pardon my ignorance—it's all thrown the same way, isn't it?"

"It may look that way," I said, "but it isn't. I can't explain it, but it's a matter of guys being more experienced and smarter and having better control and finding out more about their abilities."

"But why didn't you tell me all that?"

"I didn't know how."

"What do you mean by that?"

"I guess I was ashamed."

"Ashamed? That's nonsense. What is there to be ashamed about?"

"Well, you get down in the dumps and you don't like to talk about it."

"Not even to your father?" he asked. I couldn't tell whether he was surprised or hurt. "We've always been able to talk frankly with each other," he said. But then I saw that he didn't really believe that. A funny, slightly confused look came into his face and he turned away.

Sure, we'd always been able to talk, but it was always about things that were on his mind, things that he wanted me to be and do. It wasn't so much that we had always talked, but more that he had talked and I had listened. Wanting to go off to play ball had probably been the first time I had ever pushed a conversation, made a decision for myself.

"I don't understand your enthusiasm for baseball," he said. "I never did. You know that. All right, I can understand your love for the game. It's a nice sport. I can even understand your wanting to play when you're doing well. But to have it cause such disappointment—to the extent where you're ashamed to tell me about it—that's beyond understanding."

"A player expects that," I said. "There's a lot of disappointments, almost every day."

He shook his head.

"I still don't know why you didn't tell me about it," he said.

"I don't know either," I said. "Maybe it was because I didn't think you'd really care."

"Of course I care," he said, kind of angry I think.

"What kind of foolish talk is that? I might not know anything about curve balls, but I can certainly understand what a person is feeling—especially when he happens to be my own son."

"Well," I said, "it's more than batting averages."

He looked at me sternly.

"What's more than batting averages?" he asked.

"The way you'd think about it."

"You mean you thought I'd judge you by your *batting average?*"

That sounded dumb. I mean, you hear it said and it sounds very dumb. But somehow I couldn't help feeling that it landed pretty close to what was true.

"Ted," he said, "it makes no difference to me if you're the greatest player in the country or the worst. What has that got to do with your being my son?"

"I wanted to prove to you that I could do it."

"To me? Why to me especially?"

I didn't know why; I mean, I *did* know, but I just couldn't put it into words. Then I said, "Listen, if you had known how poorly I was doing, would you have come down here with all those people anyway?"

He started to answer, then stopped, pausing to think on it.

"I don't know," he said, very quietly. He gave me kind of a shrewd look. "I think I'm getting some of it now," he said. "Maybe you're right—maybe all of these people wouldn't have come, and maybe under any circumstances it would have been foolish to have suggested they come, unfair to you. But one thing I want you to know: *We* were coming to see you, no matter what. And by we, I mean your mother and brother and myself. As far as we're concerned, you're not a batting average, but a human being. Someone we miss, and love very much."

We walked some more, clear out to the center field fence, then toward the left field line.

"You're willing to go back to Wyattville?" he asked.

"Sure," I said.

"That won't be easy for you, since you left there as a great success."

"I've got to get more experience."

"You'll be getting more experience than you think," he said. "It's very hard to slide back like that. It won't be the same for you down there, no matter how well you do. It's going to be very hard for you."

"I know."

"There will always be people who are glad to see somebody fail."

"I know that."

"And you're willing to face it?"

"I have to," I said.

We climbed up into the grandstand and sat down.

"Not everyone would be willing to face that," he said. "Some people would rather pack it in than face humiliation."

"I'm not happy about it," I said. "But there is no choice."

"There is a choice. You can decide not to go."

I looked at him as if he had said the craziest thing.

"Not go?" I asked.

He gazed out at the field.

"I guess there's more to it than I know," he said. "I guess there's more to it than hitting a ball, or even making a living. It's more than that, isn't it? It involves pride and ambition and a dream, just like anything else, doesn't it?"

"I suppose so," I said.

"Ted, don't look on yourself as having failed," he said. "Not in any way, not as a ballplayer, not as a man. If anybody has failed, it's probably been me, for not trying to understand what all this means to you. The very fact that you're willing to go back to Wyattville and start over again makes me proud of you. It shows you've got something inside of you that has nothing to do with what other people think. The only man that can be called a failure is one who quits trying when he still has a reasonably good chance to succeed."

I'd never heard him talk like that, not to me or anybody else. It was almost like he was talking to himself, explaining to himself.

When we left the ball park we headed back to the hotel.

"What are you going to tell everybody?" I asked.

"What do you want me to tell them?"

"That I had trouble with the curve ball. That's the truth."

He laughed.

"It's highly technical," he said, "but I'll make them understand. And anyway, let them see it's not so easy; they'll appreciate it more."

"What will you do now? Gee, you've got that bus chartered and everything."

"We'll make good use of it," he said. "That's no problem. After all, there are things to see in this part of the country. We can go to Gettysburg, maybe Valley Forge." Then he got very serious. "But I'm not thinking about that."

He was walking slowly, looking down at the sidewalk, frowning. I'd seen him like that when he had some terrific legal problem he was trying to figure out. Then he stopped.

"Ted," he said, "I was just thinking. About the curve ball. Maybe if you moved up just a little closer at the bat, so you have a chance to swing at the ball before it breaks . . ." and he actually clenched his fists and put one on top of the other and lifted them into the air as though he were holding a bat.

The bus ride back to Wyattville that night was not an unhappy one at all. It should have been, but it wasn't. I was even grateful for my miserable .190 batting average, because it had done something for me that the good hitting had not—it had broken down the fences between my father and me and enabled us to talk honestly to each other for the first time.

So I curled up in my seat in the bus and as we sped through the night I read, in the thin beam of light from overhead, the book Susannah had given me, *The Science of Good Hitting*. After all, you're never too old to learn.

ABOUT THE AUTHOR

Born in Maspeth, New York, Donald Honig left home at the age of sixteen under contract to the Boston Red Sox as a pitcher. He spent the next few years playing professional ball in the South and was associated at various times with the Washington Senators and the Cincinnati Reds.

After leaving baseball he turned to writing, and though he hasn't found his ability to throw a curve ball or cover first base particularly useful in his literary career, he has published 17 books and 150 short stories over the past fifteen years. Among his most popular books for young readers are the Jed McClane stories, set in the Old West.

Mr. Honig and his wife, Sandy, now live in New York City.